Things to Do in Knoxville When You're Dead

Other Books by David Hunter

Childhood Memoirs

Trailer Trash from Tennessee
When Puppy Love Became a Howling Dog

Police Memoirs

The Moon Is Always Full
Black Friday Coming Down
There Was Blood on the Snow
The Night Is Mine
The Archangel Caper

Novels

A Whiff of Garlic
A Sonnet for Shasta
The Dancing Savior
The Jigsaw Man
Homicide Game

Co-authored with Norma Tillman

The Man With the Turquoise Eyes

Things to Do in Knoxville When You're Dead

And Other Stories

David Hunter

Tellico Books
Oak Ridge, Tennessee

Copyright © 2005 by David Hunter

Tellico Books is an imprint
of the Iris Publishing Group, Inc

Cover Photograph: Robert B. Cumming.

Design: Robert B. Cumming, Jr.

Library of Congress Cataloging-in-Publication Data

Hunter, David, 1947-
Things to do in Knoxville when you're dead : and other stories / by David Hunter.
    p. cm.
ISBN-13: 978-0-916078-80-5
ISBN-13: 978-0-916078-79-9 (pbk. : alk. paper)
ISBN-10: 0-916078-80-9
ISBN-10: 0-916078-79-5 (pbk. : alk. paper)
1. Police—Tennessee—Knoxville—Fiction. 2. Knoxville (Tenn.)—Social life and customs—Fiction. I. Title.
PS3558.U46964T48 2005
813'.54—dc22
                                                          2005028588

Acknowledgments

"Gypsy Queen With the Big Red Heart" first appeared in *Voices From the Valley*, a publication of The Knoxville Writers' Guild in October, 1994

"Daddy Hated Kudzu," first appeared in *New Millennium Writings*, Spring and Summer issue, 1996

"And Life Stands Explained" first appeared in *New Millennium Writings*, Winter Edition, 1988-1999

I dedicate this book to my longsuffering wife, Cheryl Krooss Hunter, who has loved me the same, no matter what my status.

And last of all, I honor two of the finest creatures that I've ever known: Maxie and Greta, German shepherds that lay at my feet as I wrote most of my books.

In memory of Warren Zevon (1947-2003): poet, philosopher and musician extraordinaire, whose song "Things to Do in Denver When You're Dead" inspired the title of this book.

Contents

Bounty Hunter … 9

Just Another Christmas Story … 16

Things to Do in Knoxville When You're Dead … 23

Mister Pitt's Problem … 33

Death Watch … 39

Daddy Hated Kudzu … 50

The Pretend Family Next Door … 61

The Worst Thing I Did in the War … 69

The Last Drive-in Movie … 76

Gypsy Queen With the Big Red Heart … 87

And Life Stands Explained … 95

My Doe-eyed Southern Belle … 103

Too Good to Be True … 116

Kill the Dragon, Drink Its Blood … 132

The Hands of God … 143

The Price of Safety … 153

Bounty Hunter

HANK WILLIAMS, THE long deceased—not his whiney-ass son, Bocephus—filled the air at the Blue Bird Tavern with the melancholy words of *Your Cheatin' Heart.*

There were no Kenny Chesney, Tim McGraw, Garth Brooks or Dixie Chicks songs on the antique jukebox—which still played vinyl records—just old-fashioned, unpolluted, unvarnished country music, mostly Hank Williams, Patsy Cline, George Jones, Loretta Lynn, Conway Twitty and the like.

The most recent song, put on the jukebox by a temporary employee of the company that had furnished the jukebox, and never taken off, was one by Dolly Parton, while she was still with Porter Waggoner, before she betrayed her roots and switched to mainstream music.

All along the gold-speckled Formica-topped bar were pickled eggs, pickled sausages and dill pickles in half-gallon glass jars with screw-on tops. The Bluebird's napkins featured the Kentucky Wildcats and the Tennessee Volunteer football logos, side by side. There were signed photos and posters of stars of former Kentucky and Tennessee good ol' boys who had done well on the gridiron.

The Bluebird Tavern could have been in Corbin, Kentucky, Wheeling West Virginia, Knoxville, Tennessee, Bristol, Virginia, or anywhere in the Southern Appalachian region. It wasn't, though. It was in Middletown, Ohio, between Cincinnati and Dayton.

It was that enclave of Southern Appalachian culture in Middletown that took me, a fellow hillbilly, there. An ironworker by the name of Michael Lee Bunch had jumped bail on an aggravated assault charge in Knoxville, Tennessee, my hometown, leaving my friend, bail bondsman Raford Curry, holding the bag on a fifty thousand dollar bond. I went to Middletown, hoping to find Bunch because I knew it was the closest place where he would have family *and* work. He had never done anything except ironwork since he was eighteen years old. Union ironworkers make good money. I did it for a while in my checkered youth.

My expedition was based on a SWAG. You know, a *scientific wild-assed guess*. I'm Wayne Gideon, a former cop and a current bounty hunter. Michael Bunch was worth five grand to me, ten percent of what it would cost Raford Curry if he didn't produce his wayward client pretty quickly.

A friendly union official in Knoxville had provided me with a letter to the local business agent and I had gone out on my first job as an ironworker in nearly thirty years, since my first year out of high school, when I had worked with my father the ironworker. I had forgotten how high a hundred feet *looks* from up on the steel and, at forty-six, my agility wasn't what it once was. I spent three days suffering sore, skinned knuckles and sheer terror. But I hung on because, as luck would have it, Michael Bunch was working in the same "bolt-up crew" I had been assigned to and he had found space for me where he was living.

When the steel, or red iron, as ironworkers call it, is being erected, it's hooked together by daredevils called "connectors," often referred to as "squirrels" by other ironworkers. These elite craftsmen, who defy gravity and death, catch multi-ton beams suspended from a crane on a steel cable. To bring in the beams and braces, they use a tapered wrench called a "spud" inserted in a bolt hole, to line it up with the hole in the column and put in a couple of bolts to hold it in place until the bolt-up crew follows to put in the rest of the bolts and hand-tighten them.

Afterwards, a crew with air wrenches follows and tightens the bolts down to their final thread. Once upon a time, the steel was riveted together. But even when I was following the trade, there were already few ironworkers around old enough to remember when rivets were used. In fact, there are few old iron workers, *period*. It's a dangerous occupation.

I recognized Bunch the first day. He had bleached his hair and beard and changed his name to Bill Taylor. But his fellow ironworkers still called him Stubby because he was missing the index and middle fingers from his right hand. A lot of ironworkers are missing body parts, especially fingers, because there is a tendency for novice ironworkers to stick fingers in bolt holes to see if they're lined up. That's one of the reasons it pays so well.

The trick was to get Bunch alone. The last thing I needed was a confrontation with a group of hostile men, who are not only clannish, but fear very little in this world. My patience had paid off. Bunch had invited me to the Dew Drop Inn, a "kick ass place" with "wimmen, dancin' and cheap beer, just like back home." I had been buying him one brew after another for three hours.

"Another draft beer for my friend," I told the short, slatternly bartender with the spiked green hair, ragged denim shorts, a ring through her nose and a cigarette hanging from her mouth. "You're a prins' of a guy, Shorty" Bunch said, struggling to light a cigarette. He kept missing the end with his battered Zippo lighter. "Nex' time, *I* buy."

The nickname I had adopted fit me well. I am only five-seven and with a build like a pit bull, low to the ground and heavy through the chest and arms.

I reached over and lit his cigarette. Before I could withdraw my hand, he grabbed my hand and peered closely at the lighter. It was an advertising gimmick from Bargain Bail Bonds, Raford Curry's company. A nude model adorned one side. Raford is the only man I know who is still politically incorrect enough to use such an advertisement, though it was once standard practice in the business. My heart skipped a beat. I had been careless. In the business of hunting men you can't make too many mistakes.

"Why you *sum'bitch*," Bunch said. I steeled myself for a quick exit. "We got the *same* bons'man! He gimme one a'them, but I los' it."

The tension went out of me. "Yeah, I've used old Raford a couple of times."

"Damn it. Here's to Raford!" Bunch grabbed his fresh beer, sloshing it all over the counter and lifted it in a toast. I clinked my bottled Budweiser to his mug. He chugged the whole thing, then belched loudly, following up with a, "Scuse me."

"Bill," I leaned over in a conspiratorial manner, and he moved clumsily towards me, almost falling off the stool, "I've got some cocaine back in my room. Let's go do a couple of lines."

"You got *blow*?" He put his face so close to mine that his rat's nest of curly hair and beard touched my forehead and chin. "Le's do it, then. I'll round up Bunny and High Pockets."

"No. I don't have enough for all of us. They don't have to know *everything*, do they?"

He stared at me through bloodshot brown eyes with a sly expression, then put his finger to his lips to signal silence. "You're like a fox, Shorty. Le's go."

I caught him under the arms and helped him down from the stool. As we navigated through the crowd, I saw Bunny Biggerstaff staring at us. A surly, little man, with a badly repaired cleft palate—the reason his fellow ironworkers had come up with what they considered to be a humorous and descriptive nickname—he had little to say to anyone. In particular, he had not taken to me. I pointed to the giggling, stumbling Bunch and rolled my eyes. He nodded suspiciously as we moved away, but said nothing.

Out on the street, I maneuvered Bunch to my green, '72 Volkswagen and opened the passenger door. "Did I tell you that you're a prins'?" he said.

"Yeah you told me," I replied, moving the floor mat that covered a set of leg irons, hand cuffs and a connecting chain, welded to an eye bolt in the floorboard. I closed the leg irons around his ankles. "Hold out your hands, Mister Bunch."

He complied without hesitation. Even after I snapped the cuffs on his wrists, what had just happened didn't sink into his drunken brain until I was in the car, starting the engine.

"Shorty," he said in the ponderous manner of the intoxicated, "I *try* to live and let live. I don' know where you got the wrong idea, but I'm *shtraight*. I don' even git into kinky shit with *wimmen*."

I didn't answer as I threaded my way through the back streets of the once upper middle class neighborhood, where most of the houses had been divided into apartments and boardinghouses, mostly rented to out-of-town ironworkers with jobs in Dayton. After a moment, Michael Lee Bunch, also known as Bill Taylor, had a startling epiphany.

"You called me Mister *Bunch*. You're a punk bounty hunter, *aintcha*?" Anger seemed to have made him more alert.

"That's such a harsh word, Michael Lee. These days they usually call us *bail enforcement agents*, not bounty hunters."

"I don't give a damn what they call ya. It's all the same ta me." His head tottered and saliva ran from the corner of his mouth. "I'm a *dang'rous* man, you know. Turn me loos' and I'll fergit it happened."

"For five grand, I'd go after a pit bull with AIDS—or the guy who gave him AIDS. But, since I'm not a hundred pound female, like the one you put in the hospital, I'm not really too worried about *you.*"

"Take these cuffs off and let's just see who walks away!"

"I'll do that when we get to Knoxville. But you should be sober enough by then to have better sense."

Bunch quieted down and sat sullenly, staring ahead as I pulled up in front of the rooming house where we were staying. I would have left the few clothes and toiletries behind, but my baby Glock 26, nine millimeter, was hidden under the mattress in my room. I don't have a permit to go armed in Ohio and I had decided not to carry it and risk ending up in jail over a possible random traffic stop.

I took the stairs three at a time, grabbed my small suitcase, already packed, and stuck the Glock in my hip pocket. I was inside less than five minutes, but that was enough time for Bunny and High Pockets to get home. They were standing under the street light by my VW. Through the front windshield, I could see that Bunch had a satisfied smirk on his drunken face.

"Ironworker, my ass!" Bunny Biggerstaff said as I approached, then spat on the ground. "I knowed you wasn't no ironworker." High Pockets McQuire, a hulking man with sloping shoulders and the arms of a mountain gorilla, stood beside the smaller Biggerstaff, looking grim.

Hoping to defuse the situation, I took out my badge case and showed them my tin. It was a *reserve* commission as a deputy sheriff, but good anywhere in Tennessee. Unfortunately, I wasn't in Tennessee and Bunny was smart enough to understand the difference. Before I could say anything, the disfigured little man said: "That badge ain't *shit* in Ohio. You take the chains off Stubby and we'll let you go on. You *don't*, we stomp yer ass."

They would have stomped my ass, even if I had done as ordered, just on general principles. But that wasn't going to happen, not when I already had the prisoner in hand. The pistol would probably have caused them to back off, but I couldn't chance trying to bluff two drunk ironworkers, who spent their days defying death. Shooting *anyone* was a last ditch option. I didn't want to face charges in a strange town and state.

"All right," I said. "You've got me over a barrel. Here's the key." I extended my empty hand and walked towards them, thinking, *big one first.* High Pockets' grim expression turned into a goofy smile at my apparent compliance. It was still on his face when I kicked him in the groin. He gave a sort of hissing little squeak, strange for a man his size, and fell to his knees.

Bunny Biggerstaff, though surprised, had not retreated and was holding a hawkbill pocketknife. Hawkbills are popular with ironworkers. I've never known why, but they are.

"You shouldn't bring a knife to a gunfight, Bunny," I said

"I don't see no gun." He lunged forward and I moved—a split second too late. I felt the curved blade rip into my left shoulder, which meant that Bunny hadn't kept his knife sharpened as well as he should have. You don't feel a cut from a *sharp* knife until the fight's over.

While Bunny was off balance from the slashing movement, I drove the open palm of my right hand, into his nose and felt the cartilage crunch. He staggered back and sat down, blood pouring from his nostrils. That move was taught to me back when I was a rookie cop by a man who claimed to have once been a member of the Mossad, the elite intelligence service of the Israeli government. It was probably a lie, but the move is extremely effective and doesn't leave broken knuckles.

My bantam opponent made no move to get up from his sitting position. He just sat there bubbling noisily through his nostrils. "Bunny, you probably should go to the hospital and have that nose set before the soreness sets in. And Highpockets, I hope I didn't do any permanent damage."

The big man was still on his knees, rocking from side to side in agony, but his diminutive friend responded with an angry glare as I got in my car and drove away from the curb. It was possible Bunny would call the police, but not likely. I had humiliated the two of them and they understood that even if the local police stopped us, Bunch would still have to go back to Knoxville now because I had a paper on him that said I could take him across a state line without a warrant. The FBI can't do that but a bounty hunter can.

"Bunny *cutcha*, didn' he?" Bunch said with a sneer.

"I'll quit bleeding before *he* does. Now sit back and shut up before I work on *your* face, you woman-beating son-of-a-bitch!" My shoulder was throbbing, but the bleeding stopped pretty quickly. Bunch did as I had told him, and a few minutes later he was snoring, sleeping off his last drunk for a while.

By the time he stirred again, I was driving across the bridge over the Ohio River into Kentucky. And as any hillbilly will tell you, Cincinnati is the most beautiful city in America—when seen from the rearview mirror of a southbound car.

Just Another Christmas Story

"UNIT 17, SEE the party at 2120 Dorshire regarding a dead body."

"Ten-4," Officer Charlie Quick responded. *A dead body.* Had the Lord of the Manor, the fat, wheezing bully, finally killed somebody? And on Christmas Eve? Quick had been to that address often enough to recognize it instantly. It was always the same—a neighbor would call in a disturbance, and he would arrive to find broken furniture and battered family members.

Casting fearful glances at Sonny Boy Bleu—his honest-to-God given name—the wife and her two elderly parents would deny that there had been any problem, despite bruises and swollen faces.

With no complaint, police action could not be taken. When Bleu would order him from the house, as he always did, Officer Charlie Quick had no choice but to leave because the state had no domestic violence law at the time. The bullying man's smugness had become a thorn in the officer's side.

Which one had Bleu finally killed? Was it his wife, a frail thin woman of forty or so with mousy brown hair? Or was it her father, silver-haired and confined to a wheelchair from a degenerative spinal disease. Quick sincerely hoped it wasn't the mother, a distinguished-looking woman of seventy, who wore an elegant, old-fashioned red beret and sat proudly with shoulders back, even though she was obviously afraid of her son-in-law.

Quick had been on the same beat for six years. When Sonny Boy Bleu was still a long distance truck driver, the abuse had only occurred every few months. After he had been disabled by high blood pressure and heart disease, the complaints had become a monthly event. Within a year, the neighbors were calling in at least once a week, sometimes more often.

Retired from his job, Sonny Bleu had nothing to do but drink, watch television and beat up on people who couldn't fight back—and he enjoyed it.

Within five minutes, Quick turned his cruiser up the long driveway to the Bleu residence. It was a neat, frame house in a working class neighborhood. A sad attempt at Christmas decoration had been made by stringing lights on a small shrub by the front porch. A few old-fashioned Christmas lights, the big bulbs that hadn't been sold in years, shown dimly, with most of the lights carelessly bunched on one side.

Sonny Boy Bleu's late model red pickup truck, the only vehicle owned by the family, was parked in the driveway There were two bumper stickers on the truck: One said, *Abortion is murder*, the other proclaimed, *I am a Vietnam Vet*. Quick knew the latter was a lie because he had checked. Sonny had been a mail clerk at Fort Benning, Georgia and had never left the United States.

The husky, medium tall officer got out of his car and walked up the front steps, a knot tightening in his stomach. Death is not a thing any sane person ever gets used to, despite what films and television cop shows seem to indicate He knocked and a moment later, Bleu's wife opened the door. "Please come in, Officer Quick."

Quick was startled; she had never invited him in before, though he had pushed his way past her many time, hoping to Catch Sonny Boy in the act. He glanced over her shoulder and saw that Sonny Boy was in his lounge chair. Mrs. Bleu's elderly parents were in their usual places—the mother on the couch and the father sitting near her in his wheel chair.

"Then, who…" Quick started to ask.

Mrs. Bleu nodded towards the recliner before Quick's words were out of his mouth. "It's my husband. "He died," she said matter-of-factly.

Charlie Quick walked past her and around in front of the chair. Bleu's head was back, his mouth and eyes were open in what is sometimes called the rictus smile. He was definitely dead, but Charlie went through the motions, automatically checking for a pulse and pupil response.

"I'll have to write a report and call the medical examiner," Quick said. "Would you like me to get a sheet or blanket and cover him up?"

"If you want to," Mrs. Bleu said. "But I'm all right." The Christmas tree, flashing in multi-hued colors, lent an air of surrealism to the scene.

The officer turned and looked at the elderly parents. Both shrugged, seemingly unconcerned, so Charlie went back to his cruiser and got a pad of blank offense reports. None of them were pretending that they were upset over Bleu's death. *That's good,* the veteran cop thought. He didn't think Bleu would be missed, and he hated hypocrisy. Still, unexpected death stirs up emotions, even when a tyrant dies. Where were the emotions? In a moment the officer was back in the house.

"I'll try to hurry," Quick said, sitting down in a threadbare cloth-covered chair, opposite the wife and her parents, by the Christmas tree. "I know this is a difficult time. He penned in the date, *December 24*, the year and then *Bleu, Sonny Boy* on the top line of the form. "How old was your husband?"

"He was 56 on March 1st," she answered.

"Do you know his Social Security number?

She reeled it off from memory.

"Who was his doctor?"

"Doctor John Dew," she replied.

"Exactly what was your husband's medical condition?"

"He had heart disease, high blood pressure, diabetes, and a disintegrating disk in his lower back."

"Can you tell me about what time…that is, did you notice when …" Charlie Quick stumbled over the wording of his question.

"He threw back his head and gasped, then quit breathing at *exactly* eleven o'clock, the elderly mother said. "The news was just coming on."

"That's right," Mrs. Bleu said. The elderly man with silver hair nodded affirmatively.

"Was he doing anything strenuous that might have strained his heart?"

"Sonny Boy Blue doing something *strenuous*?" the elderly mother said scornfully. "The heaviest thing he ever lifted was a can of beer."

"He ate his steak and eggs, like he did every night," the thin, drawn Mrs. Bleu said. "Then he told me to fix him some eggnog. He usually has a chocolate milkshake after supper, but he likes eggnog at Christmas time. I fixed it. He drank it and died a few minutes later.

Quick glanced at the table beside Bleu's chair and saw the empty plate and glass. "Was he the only one who had dinner?"

"He *never* ate with us. We had our dinner an hour earlier." Mrs. Bleu said.

"Yeah," the old man spoke for the first time. "We always had our beans and cornbread, potato soup or beef stew if *he* was in a generous mood when he shopped, and he had his steak and eggs or sometimes pork tenderloin every night."

Charlie Quick raised an eyebrow and looked at Mrs. Bleu.

"Sonny always got what he wanted," she said. "We ate on the cheap because he said it was all he could afford."

"Didn't you complain?" The question was not pertinent to the report, but the officer's curiosity was piqued. He had apparently seen only the tip of the iceberg in his calls to the house.

"He made us sign our Social Security checks over to him every month. And since *he* was the only one who could drive, *he* decided everything You *know* what happened whenever one of us complained. You were here often enough," the elderly mother said, accusingly.

"Ma'am, I did what the law allowed me." It sounded lame, even to Charlie Quick.

"I guess there's something wrong with the law," the father said.

"I guess so," the officer replied, then went on before anything else could be said. "I need to know what kind of medications your husband was taking "

"They're on the counter in the kitchen. All of them."

Charlie went to the counter, just inside the kitchen, which opened into the living room without doors, and began to laboriously record the medication and dosage on each amber bottle from Walgreens. He was familiar with most of them.

When came to the last bottle, the officer noted that it was a hydrocodone, a fairly heavyweight painkiller. He was about to set it back down when he saw that a prescription for thirty had been filled that day. The bottle was empty,

A suspicion crept into Charlie's mind. He tried to dismiss it but it held on like an embedded tick and loomed larger every moment that he stood with the empty medicine bottle in his hand. He went back into the living room.

"Mrs. Bleu, was your husband complaining with his back? Was he maybe taking an excessive number of pain pills today?" The elderly couple quickly glanced at each other. Mrs. Bleu did not take the avenue that Officer Charlie Quick was offering.

"Not that I know of," she said.

Quick looked at the glass from which the eggnog been consumed. Then he glanced at the blender in the sink, still coated with the viscous yellow liquid. When Quick turned back, all three were staring directly at him. Waiting. Suddenly Charlie quick understood clearly, for the first time in his life, the meaning of pregnant silence.

"I...Would you excuse me for a moment? I have to get something out of the car," Charlie said. The three of them nodded, but said nothing.

Outside in the crisp, cold darkness, on the eve of Christ's birthday, one he knew would be as clear in his mind thirty years later as it was at that moment, Charlie Quick took out a cigarette and lit it with trembling hands. He took a long drag and held the smoke in his lungs. Inside the house, three people were waiting for him to make a decision that would change the course of their lives.

If he reported his suspicions, the homicide detectives would come and take the blender and glass to the laboratory for analysis. They would find—Charlie had no doubt—massive quantities of the narcotic painkiller in the residual eggnog. There would be at least one more arrest, a hearing and a trial. Sonny Boy's wife would go to prison and her elderly parents to a nursing home. *But to what good?*

Charlie Quick had been a cop since he was eighteen. First as a military police officer, then ten years as a sheriff's deputy. He had never wanted to do anything else. He was an officer of the law who had never taken a penny that wasn't rightfully his. Nor had he ever looked the other way, not even for friends or family. The slippery slope leading to a yawning abyss was now before him.

Like most good cops, Charlie Quick, known to his cop friends as *Quick* Charlie Quick because of his ability to see what others often missed, had given up the quest for justice two years into the job. Instead, he had striven for impartial enforcement of the law—at least on his part—and had succeeded. But *justice* was another breed of cat altogether.

There was no justice in allowing a man like Sonny Boy Bleu to torment and abuse helpless people. But he had done it for years—and gotten away with it while good men like Charlie left the house, time after time in impotent rage at their inability to help those who could not help themselves.

The three people in the house were no threat to anyone else. Charging them with murder and conspiracy would serve no useful purpose. *Still,* Charlie thought, *murder has been a crime ever since the Garden of Eden.* It had been forbidden by the Ten Commandments, Hammurabbi's Code, and most especially, by the law of the sovereign state of Tennessee—which Charlie Quick had sworn to uphold.

He reached for his portable radio and keyed it. "Unit 17, have the coroner call me at this location."

"Ten-4, Unit 17." The dispatcher replied.

Charlie opened the door and went back into the house where the three people waited. He said: "The coroner will be calling very soon and I'll finish up as quickly as I can."

They all nodded, glancing at each other, but said nothing. They had put their fate in Charlie Quick's hands. *Damn them!* What right did they have to involve him in a felony? And especially on Christmas Eve.

After what seemed hours of silence, but was less than five minutes, the phone rang. Charlie went to the table beside Sonny Boy Bleu's chair and answered it.

"Officer Quick," he said.

"This is Doctor Franklin, Officer Quick. What do you have?"

"I have a white male, 56 years of age, morbidly obese with a history of heart disease, diabetes and spinal problems. He was a heavy drinker, was on hydrocodone for pain and his last meal was steak, eggs and eggnog."

"Sounds like a no-brainer," the coroner chuckled. "Do you see any indication of foul play?"

Officer Charlie Quick stood looking at the three other people in the room. All of them were waiting quietly, staring at him. Seconds passed.

"Are you still there, Officer Quick?"

"Yes, I'm still here."

"Do you see any indication of foul play?"

"No," Charlie said. "Everything looks kosher."

"Then release the body to the funeral home of the family's choice. And have a Merry Christmas, Officer Quick"

"Thank you, and a Merry Christmas to you." The phone went

dead on the other end. Charlie put the receiver in its cradle and once again picked up his radio. "Which funeral home would you prefer," he asked.

"Wilkerson's," Mrs. Bleu said.

Charlie Quick radioed for the hearse, then turned to the three people again. "You need to clean up your dishes and throw your husband's medicine away, since he doesn't need it any longer. Do you *understand* what I'm saying?"

Mrs. Bleu, nodded without speaking, got up immediately, and picked up the plate and glass from the table beside her husband, without even glancing at the body. She rinsed them off, along with the blender, put them in the dishwasher and turned it on. A moment later, Charlie could hear the soap and water hissing and steaming inside the machine, eradicating evidence.

The elderly mother gathered up the medicine bottles, put them in a paper bag and took it out the back door. He heard a metal lid clang on a garbage can.

"I'll wait on the porch," he told them, "until the hearse comes."

That's where Charlie Quick was standing, smoking his third cigarette, when the Cadillac hearse arrived from the funeral home. The crew was very efficient. They had a lot of experience with death and it's protocol. They murmured their condolences and five minutes later, Sonny Boy Bleu was gone. Within hours his veins would be full of embalming fluid.

Officer Charlie Quick finished a fourth cigarette and flipped it out into the yard. He was about to go to his cruiser, when the door opened again. It was the elderly mother.

"We're going to fix a late Christmas snack, steak and eggs. Would you like to join us, Officer Quick?"

"I don't think so," Charlie said, "but I appreciate the offer."

"Anytime you're in the neighborhood, stop by. You're always welcome here. You've always been very kind." She lifted her right hand and tucked a wisp of white hair under the red beret.

"Merry Christmas, Officer Quick," the elderly woman called after him, but Charlie didn't look back.

Things to Do in Knoxville When You're Dead

WARREN ZEVON WAS singing the last verse of *Things to Do in Denver When You're Dead* from the movie soundtrack of the same name when I passed the naked woman in the fog. There was almost an ethereal look to her as she strode purposefully forward beside the highway, staring straight ahead. I immediately braked but by the time I brought my car to a complete halt, the fog had enclosed her once more.

I sat and watched in my rearview mirror, waiting for her to emerge from the fog as the final notes of the song played out. My Warren Zevon music goes with me everywhere. Most people don't even know who he was unless they heard one of his sound tracks such as the one I was playing from the movie about Denver gangsters—with Andy Garcia, Gabrielle Anwar and Christopher Walken. He also did the sound track and title song for *Werewolves of London.*

A few moments went by and I almost doubted that I had really seen her. I sell police equipment and I've had cops tell me about times when they'd seen things they couldn't believe they had seen until they went back and looked again. On dark roads at night, the eyes can play tricks. But a moment later, she appeared in my rear-view mirror, out of the fog, still walking purposefully, eyes straight ahead.

She was perhaps thirty, but a young thirty. Her full breasts moved up and down with every step and had remarkably little droop for a woman of her build—at least one past the age of nineteen. Her hair was long and dark, brunette or auburn. She was wearing high heels and carrying a large, black purse over her shoulder.

I got out of the car and walked around to the passenger side. When she was within three feet of me she stopped and looked in my eyes without comprehension. She was absolutely beautiful and I tried not to stare down at her breasts, though the temptation was almost irresistible.

"Miss…are you all right?" It was lame, I knew. Her eyes focused on my face.

"I need help," she said. *Obviously in shock,* I thought. Her accent was soft and elegant like dialogue from a movie about the Old South. Well, I *was* in Tennessee. How else would she speak?

"Get in the front seat and I'll find something to wrap around you."

"All right," she replied. I opened the passenger side door and she got in, clutching her purse closely. That was when I noticed what appeared to be flecks of blood all over her breasts and stomach. I had always wondered how I would react to a *real* crisis. Selling police supplies does not present a lot of opportunities for adventure, other than the vicarious kind.

There was no blanket in the trunk, but I had a sports jacket, still in the plastic wrap from the dry-cleaners, laid out over my suitcase.

"Here," I said, standing by the open car door again, extending the jacket. She didn't put out her hands to take it, so I touched her shoulder lightly. She leaned forward and I draped the jacket over her shoulders. "There you go," I said. I saw that her hair was a deep shade of auburn.

"Can you tell me what happened?" I asked, getting back into the car. *Oh my God. Would the question push her over the edge? Incredibly stupid,* I told myself.

"No," she replied. The jacket had not covered her full breasts and they thrust forward from the jacket like the noses of inquisitive puppies. I realized I was staring again. *Stop it! This woman is in shock and staring is like psychic rape.* "I don't know what happened. I came to myself walking along the highway."

I pulled back on the road and a chill of uncertainty ran down my spine, as if someone had just walked over my grave—or the way it would feel, if I had a grave. Of course, it was the excitement that caused the chill. That I was even off the interstate was an adventure to a traveling salesman. I had taken a detour to get around a traffic accident because I was in a hurry. *How long would dealing with this woman delay me? Bastard, it makes no difference. You have to help!*

We drove along in silence for a brief time. I was fearful of asking any further questions. I would stop in the next town of any size and take her to a hospital. That's what I'd do. But I was not familiar with this back road section of Tennessee, and had no idea what the next town would be. For that matter, I wasn't sure what the *last* town had been. I tend to zone out, go on autopilot during long drives.

"I seem to have splattered something on myself," she said, opening her large, purse. She stared into it for a moment, then took a shiny, silver-looking revolver from the purse and sat holding it by the checkered grip with two fingers, as if she had taken a snake in her hand.

I pulled over as smoothly as I could, trying to watch the road and the pistol at the same time. The only thing I really knew about guns was that they killed people. Once I was stopped, I took the pistol from her hand. She was still staring at it and didn't resist as I gingerly gripped the barrel with my left hand, then transferred it to my right hand and slid it under my seat.

"I'm, Joe Pruitt, from Indianapolis," I said, trying to distract her thoughts from the pistol as I pulled back on to the road again. "I sell police supplies—uniforms, leather and other equipment." She had begun to rummage in her purse again and seemed disinterested in what I had to say.

"I don't seem to have a tissue," she said, "and I've spattered myself with something."

"I'll stop at the first place we come to and get you something to clean up with. It shouldn't be too far."

"You're very kind," she said.

"This fog has been a killer tonight," I said. *Damn! Just the thing to say to a woman with blood spattered on her breasts and belly. Keep it up, Pruitt!*

"Yes, the fog is worse than usual tonight," she answered.

"I wouldn't have been out on the highway in the wee hours of the morning if I didn't have a sales meeting in Cincinnati this afternoon," I told her. "I left Chattanooga on I-75, then got off the interstate to go around an accident.

"We live near Chattanooga. I really don't know why *we* were out tonight."

"Who is we?" *Foot in mouth again.* I seemed determined to drive her into hysterics.

She turned those dark eyes toward me inquisitively. "I don't really know, Mister…?" she waited.

"Pruitt. Joe Pruitt," I told her for the second time.

"Forgive me, I don't seem to be myself tonight." She turned her head from side to side, as if trying to loosen her neck muscles.

"Don't worry about it. Things have a way of working themselves out." *Don't worry!* My social skills had vanished altogether in the presence of her magnificent body, but she didn't seem to have noticed. *Dear, God, please let me get her to a hospital before she really wakes up!*

An interstate ramp sign was suddenly looming ahead. I breathed a sigh of relief as I took the northbound on-ramp. There would surely be a hospital close by. This was Tennessee, after all, not outer Mongolia. The fog had cleared a little and I was able to speed up.

"How do we know each other, Mister Pruitt?" Her expression was like that of an inquisitive but bewildered child.

"You…you needed a ride and I stopped and offered you one." She nodded, as if satisfied with the answer.

"The fog seems to be lifting. What time is it, Mister Pruitt?"

"It's a little after three," I said, once more fighting to keep my eyes off her breasts on which the nipples were suddenly standing at attention, as if she had chilled.

"I have no idea why we were out as this hour of the morning. Do you know, Mister Pruitt?"

"No, you didn't tell me. But I'm sure there was a good reason." *Keep her calm.* "Here's a sign for a service station, now." I took the exit slowly. *Maybe there would be a cop at the service station. That was a silly thought, you never see a cop when you need one—not even when you sell police supplies for a living.*

It was an Exxon station and there were no other cars. As soon as I stopped by the end of the building near the sign that said "rest rooms," she opened the car door and stepped out. The jacket fell from her shoulders and she was once more naked, except for the high heels and purse. A young man, mouth open, stared from inside. I quickly got out and picked up the jacket, just as she closed the restroom door.

After a what seemed an eternity, but was probably only five minutes, the young clerk came out. He was eighteen or nineteen, with a sprinkling of acne on his cheeks. He looked at me with a puzzled and somewhat fearful expression. "Is your wife all right, Mister?"

"Would you call the police?" I said.

"To tell the truth, I already *tried* to call the police when I saw her walking around nekkid, but the phone's not workin' for some reason.

Don't you have a cell phone?" the young man asked, looking at the rented Oldsmobile, probably certain a man in an expensive car should have a cell phone.

"I left it at a restaurant in Alabama," I told him. Before he could respond, the woman came out of the restroom and walked towards the car. I met her and put the jacket around her shoulders again. I saw that she hadn't cleaned herself up. The blood, if it was blood, was still spattered on her breasts and flat stomach.

"Where's the closest hospital," I asked the clerk.

He took a moment to answer because his eyes were on the woman, whose breasts had jutted out of my jacket again as she got into the car. "It's about twenty or thirty miles south. Be the third exit, I think. There's a sign." I was pretty sure he had not been focused on giving directions. As we drove away, he stood watching.

"Where did you pick me up, Mister Pruitt? She asked.

"I really don't know. I had gotten off the interstate to avoid an accident that had the road blocked. I couldn't see much in the fog." She seemed to accept my answer.

"So, it was fate that brought you to me, Mister Pruitt. That happens."

I was fearful of asking the wrong question, so I drove along without responding, counting the exits. When I arrived at the third exit, sure enough there was a hospital sign. I turned on the blinker.

"*What are you doing?*" Her eyes opened wide.

"I was going to take you by the hospital...."

"No, no, no, *not* the hospital. *Please don't stop!*" She grabbed the steering wheel and I almost lost control. By the time I had the car steadied, we had passed the exit.

"Ma'am, why are you afraid of the hospital?"

"My name is Sharon..." she seemed startled to have remembered. "They'll kill my husband if I go to a hospital."

"*Who* will kill your husband?" Suddenly *I* was really nervous.

"The men who have him..." She turned to stare with those beautiful, dark eyes. "They said I couldn't tell or they would kill him. Please, just let me ride with you a little longer."

"All right. Calm down. We'll work things out." I told her. We drove in silence for ten minutes or so. It was a bad situation, I knew. I was driving on a major interstate with a beautiful, naked woman in my car, a pistol under my seat—and I had no idea *how* she had come to be spattered with what looked like blood. Despite everything else, my eyes kept drifting to that near-perfect body.

"Mister Pruitt, would you stop at the next service station? I'm sorry but I need to use the restroom again."

"Sure. There's an exit coming up. We'll pull off." *Maybe there would be a working telephone.*

The exit was dark, except for a sign that said BP, a few hundred yards to the left of the exit ramp. It was a combination convenience store and gas station, like the last one. I stopped near the restroom again and she got out, once more leaving the coat behind. *My God her body was beautiful!*

I got out of the rented Olds and walked through door into the well-lit convenience store. There was no clerk in sight and no pay phone visible, but there was fresh coffee. I was taking the first sip from a Styrofoam cup when the elderly man came out of the back.

"Sorry neighbor, I was takin' out the trash. I see you found the coffee." He was wearing a white shirt and black bowtie with a red vest.

"Can you tell me the name of the next city of any size? I'm northbound."

"That would be Knoxville."

"Do you have a phone I can use?" I asked.

"I got one but it's just for business and emergencies. You got an emergency?" he asked. "If you do…" His voice trailed off and eyes stared past me. "Mister, there's a stark naked woman standing at the door. Do you know her?"

As I turned, she opened the door and asked,. "Are you ready to go?"

"Yes, I'll be right there." She turned and walked to my rental car. I watched entranced, in spite of myself—until she went to the driver's side and opened the door.

"I have to go," I sloshed hot coffee over my hand as I rushed outside.

"Hey mister, ya didn't pay for that coffee," the old man yelled at me.

In the car, she was fumbling for the ignition switch. I touched her arm doing my best not to frighten her. "Sharon, I'll drive."

"All right, Mister Pruitt." She slid across the leather seat to the passenger side. "We need to leave, they may catch up with us if we don't keep moving."

"Who are you talking about, Sharon?"

"Please get us out of here, quickly, Mister Pruitt!"

"All right, stay calm, Sharon." I started the car and pulled away, spilling more hot coffee on my already stinging hand.

"The coffee smells good, Mister Pruitt."

"Would you like some?" I extended the cup and she took it from my hand, sipped carefully and handed it back.

"Thank you, Mister Pruitt. You're very kind."

Once more, we drove in silence. I was doing my best not to cast lingering glances at her. In fifteen minutes or so, I passed a place called Rockwood. I had decided to go on to Knoxville, certain I could find a police car there. I found myself once more leering at the poor, disturbed woman's nearly naked body. I put the Warren Zevon CD on and we drove in silence for a while. I tried to keep my eyes straight ahead, not with complete success.

"It looks like we're almost to Knoxville, Sharon. It's a fairly big town. You can probably trust the police there not to be in on whatever happened to you and your husband back down the highway."

"You're right, Mister Pruitt. Maybe it's time to contact the police. Maybe they're even looking for us by now."

I started to ask what she meant, but I didn't because I was immensely relieved that she seemed to be making a little sense. And by that time all I really wanted was for someone to take her off my hands.

Even though I had been hoping to see a police car, it was a surprise when the blue lights started flashing behind me just inside Knoxville, beyond the first truck stop where the interstate became four lanes. I didn't know what traffic law I had broken, but I didn't care either. *They can take this woman off my hands and I'll be on my way with a clear conscience*, I thought.

Easing over to the shoulder, I said: "Well Sharon, it looks the police have found *us*."

"Yes it does, Mister Pruitt. You're a very nice man and I'm sorry you were the one who picked me up. But things are out of my control now," she said.

"What do you mean, Sharon?" She seemed to be making less sense than she had a moment before. But I got no answer because she opened the car door, leaving the sports jacket behind, and ran back towards the police car—her beautiful, heart shaped ass, a wonder to behold—screaming as she went. I sat stunned by the turn of events until I heard the police intercom.

"Put both hands out the window," the metallically enhanced voice boomed out, "or I will shoot you."

I quickly put my hands out the window as I was told and saw that a second set of blue lights was suddenly flashing behind the first. Then, yet another set of lights arrived. *How many cops does it take to stop a traffic violator?* I thought.

"Open the car door from the outside with your *right* hand. Do it now or we will shoot!" The voice boomed again. *I* had ominously become *we.*

"Now get out with your back to us. Lock your fingers behind your head and walk slowly backwards. Do it now!" There was no way I was going to further upset an obviously nervous cop. I've heard too many horror stories from my customers to make *that* mistake. I gingerly got out and did as I was told. We'd straighten things out when everyone was calm.

"Lie face down with your arms straight out to the side and your palms up. Do it now!"

A moment later, after doing as I was ordered, I felt a knee in the small of my back and a handcuff closing on my right wrist. "If you move, scumbag, I'll blow your head off. Put the other hand behind you!"

As he closed the other handcuff on my left wrist, I said: "Officer, I *know* how this must look, but I have a reasonable explanation."

"I just bet you do," the officer said, picking me up by the collar and slamming me against the trunk of my rental car I felt his hands roughly moving over my body in an impersonal manner I hadn't experienced since my Army physical twenty years earlier.

A female officer in a navy uniform, a patch that said Knoxville Police Department on the shoulder, walked past me and the officer who had handcuffed me.

She bent down and reached under the front seat of the Oldsmobile. She came out with the silver-looking pistol, holding it by the rough grips with two fingers, the way the woman had held it earlier. I had seen enough cop movies to know that the officer was being careful not to smear any prints that might be on the pistol. Suddenly the knot of apprehension in my stomach got much larger than it had been.

"That's not *my* pistol," I said.

"And I bet we won't find your prints on it, will we?" The female officers's accent flattened all the vowels. She dropped the pistol into a manila envelope I hadn't seen in her hands. It was marked "evidence.".

"Yes you will, but…"

"You're one dumb sumbitch, Pruitt," the first officer said. You blow a man away because he tries to stop you from rapin' his wife. Then you drive another fifty miles, let a naked woman spattered with her husband's blood out to use the restroom *twice*, in front of witnesses— *then* steal a cup of coffee that cost about a dollar. Dumb sumbitch, I'm telling ya. Didn't it occur to you that an intelligent woman might leave messages in the restrooms?"

"She was in shock and I was trying to keep her calm," I told him. "I found her back on a country road, walking along naked."

"Well, she wasn't so much in shock that she couldn't write messages on the restroom mirrors with her lipstick the two times you stopped— and you lied to the clerk at the first place and *said* she was your wife."

"No, it wasn't like that. He just *assumed* she was my wife and I didn't have time to argue. And I *didn't* steal the coffee at the last stop. I just left in a hurry because I was afraid Sharon was about to drive off in my car."

"So now she's Sharon. You have an answer for everything, don't you? Now let's move!" Holding me by the scruff of the neck again, the walked me past the first cruiser which was marked Knoxville Police Department. The woman was sitting in the back, covered with a blanket, tears running down her face.

"Ask her," I said, trying to stop by the cruiser where she sat. She looked up, with what appeared to be terror in her eyes and tried to move away from the door. *She's still in shock,* I thought. *When she comes around she'll tell them what happened.*

Then, just as the officer shoved me past the car window, her look of fear was replaced by pity, for just a fleeting second. It was brief. Not enough for the officers to notice—even if they had been watching— but enough to let me know that she *wasn't* in shock and *hadn't* been. She had played me.

Everything was suddenly coming to me with perfect, terrifying clarity. An officer at a sales meeting in New York had once told me about a training exercise in which a woman with her breasts almost bare, wearing a low-cut blouse, managed to shoot every cop who approached the car she was in, even though the pistol was in plain sight on the car seat when they walked up. Just her *cleavage* had distracted trained police officers long enough to have gotten them killed in a real situation. I hadn't stood a chance.

What had she said just before she got out of my car, screaming. "You're a very nice man and I'm sorry you were the one who picked me up. But things are out of my control now." *For me, things had been out of my control since the moment I first saw her naked body!*

I wondered how long she had waited for a patsy like me to come down the road after she shot her husband to death. Probably not very long. *What ruse had she used to get out of her clothing to distract her husband. Maybe a quickie by the side of the road? It didn't really matter, though. Once she had gotten out of them, he was probably too distracted to even see the pistol until she began to pull the trigger.*

The officer who had me by the collar opened a rear cruiser door. He put his hand on top of my head, the way it's done in the cop shows, so I wouldn't hurt myself as I got in. I saw that there were no handles or locks inside and it was a shock, even though I knew police cars had no locks in the backseat cage. I'd never seen a cruiser door from the inside.

I also knew—with a horrible clarity—that I would not be giving a sales presentation in Cincinnati later in the day. The Knoxville officers would call the county where I had found the woman and I would be charged with the commission of a felony—several in fact. Most likely, I would never leave Tennessee again.

Who would ever believe a preposterous story like mine, told by a Yankee outsider, over the testimony of a classy, beautiful hometown woman, who had just become a widow?

They would believe *her*—even when she told the story fully clothed.

Mister Pitt's Problem

"Do you remember that nigger lawyer, Robert Pitt?" Walt Godfrey asked Gordon Wallace, as he and his friend clocked out for lunch. "You know, the one who looked like Calhoun from the old *Amos 'n Andy Show*. He was a lawyer, too—I mean, his *character* was."

Of medium height, gone bald on top, Walt had once worn a hairstyle reminiscent of Elvis Presley in his heyday. At sixty-five, with shoulders stooping, a bald spot like a monk's tonsure and paunch still growing, it was hard to believe that his coworkers had once called him The Tennessee Stud.

"Yeah, I remember him," Gordon Wallace answered. One of the first nigger lawyers in Knoxville. Used to defend a lot of whores. Come to think of it, he once got a soul brother off a dope charge I'd put on him. Let's see...the doper was called Sweet Meat Brown. A disk jockey for that blues station that used to be on Magnolia Avenue. You remember Sweet Meat?"

"No, but I remember the radio station. There was always fresh coffee when we went by. And they always treated us respectful."

"Yeah," Gordon said with a shake of his head, "I'd almost forgotten about that soul station." Chunky, red hair shot with silver and with a third jowl forming, Gordon Wallace bore little resemblance to the lean, hard street cop he had once been. "Seems like just yesterday, don't it? Time sure gets away quick."

"Yeah, you're right," Godfrey replied. "Things *do* seem to get away. There was a time when I never forgot a name or a face. Hell, we didn't have computers to do our thinking for us, did we? No sir. Cops startin' out in our day had to do *real* police work."

The two of them had been together thirty years, longer than most marriages last. In fact, they had gone through five marriages between them and both were presently single.

They had decided to pull the pin and get out after twenty-five years with the Knoxville Police Department so that they could spend more time on recreation. Both had sworn they would never become bailiffs at the court house, the place where retired officers often went for a second career.

Circumstances had changed their minds, however. The really good jobs in industrial security were all snapped up by retired federal agents and police chiefs with better education and contacts, and the two retired sergeants had found that golf palled quickly and that the boating season lasted longer than their interest in boating. Finally, after a year of leisure, they had signed on as bailiff's, working court security. It was better than nothing.

"What were you sayin' about Robert Pitt?" Gordon asked.

"I just asked if you remembered him?"

"Yeah, I do. I said that, didn't I?"

"I don't remember—but anyway, the other day..."

"Godfrey, Wallace. Come back! Fight in the court room!" A deputy clerk in a red and white polka dot dress yelled from the back hallway door.

They hurried to the courtroom and found their relief officer (at seventy-six, the oldest bailiff in the court system) ineffectually trying to pull a young man with straw-colored hair off an older man stretched out on the floor. The victim's lips were turning blue as the younger man's fingers closed more and more tightly.

"Let go!" Wallace yelled, grabbing the young man by the hair and pulling his head backwards. Godfrey reached down and probed under the young man's armpit. When he drove his thumb into the underlying nerve, there was a grunt from the attacker and a gasp of breath from the man on the floor under him.

Moments later, several blue suits from the jail division poured off the elevator and swarmed the young assailant who was lying on the floor sobbing.

"You guys all right?" a crew cut jailer wearing sergeant chevrons on his collar asked.

"Why *wouldn't* we be all right?" Wallace asked. "We was both out there fightin' crime before *you* were born!"

"No offense meant," the jail sergeant said. He was a big man with the arms of a weight-lifter and a broad, ruddy face.

"None taken," Godfrey said. "We're goin' on to lunch." Put us down as witnesses, if you have to."

Outside in the hall, Wallace turned to his aging partner. "Something ought to be done about these old farts who can't hold up their end anymore. Cleaver was a cop when *I* was a kid."

"You mean the old bailiff?" Godfrey asked.

"Yeah, he was a cop over in Blount County and he retired a *long* time ago," Wallace said. "He's way too old to be wrestling with kids."

"I'd say that's how that young jail sergeant feels about us," Godfrey said.

"Naw. It ain't the same thing. We've still got a lot of fire left," Wallace replied.

"I'm sixty-five," Godfrey said with a shake of his head, and you're a year older than I am. My hair's all gone off the top and yours is almost white."

"Get on with your story about the nigger lawyer." Gordon Wallace quickly changed the subject. He was sensitive about his silver-streaked hair.

"Well, you remember back when he first started…" Godfrey began, but was interrupted yet again by a voice at the top of the stairs.

"My Lord, as I live and breathe. It's the Lone Ranger and Tonto —the fastest zippers at the Knoxville Police Department."

"Look here, Walt," Gordon Wallace said, smiling at the woman who had spoken, a smile pulling all three of his jowls upward, "it's Big Ellie."

"Bigger, blacker and more beautiful than ever," she said. Ellie was a large woman in her early sixties with a pale and badly mottled complexion. Despite that, the black suede coat with an ermine collar gave her a majestic air.

"What are you up here for, Ellie? Surely to God you ain't still turnin' tricks" Walt Godfrey said.

"Of course not! I am a *businesswoman,* and a respected member of the community, but I could still bring in the money if I wanted to. My niece got in a little trouble last night and I'm here to bail her out."

"Your *niece* didn't happen to get picked up for solicitin', did she?" Wallace asked with a wink.

"No. Silly, little bitch was driving drunk last night. Say, you two couldn't help her out, could you?"

"No," Godfrey said. "We ain't got that kind of clout no more."

"Too bad. If you could help her out, I'd send a couple of girls over to make it worth your effort—if you know what I mean."

"Yeah, we do," Walt said. "But we both gave up the strange stuff when AIDS came along in the eighties. It was good to see you again, Ellie, but we're on our way to lunch." The older the two got, the more important lunch at a regular time became. It had become an important ritual since retirement. Before, when they were on the streets, food had only been something to be grabbed on the run between adventures.

"Things sure has changed," the big woman said wistfully. "Yawl be careful, ya hear?" She turned with a wave of her trademark purple silk scarf and a whiff of honeysuckle as she walked away. For a moment, it took the two of them back in time.

"That Ellie was something else when we first went out on patrol wasn't she?" Godfrey said.

"Yeah, that gal could suck golf balls through a one inch garden hose when she was young." Wallace laughed. "You gonna get a hot sandwich or somethin' from the cooler?"

They had arrived at the coffee shop on the first floor of the City-County Building.

"I think I'll just have a soft drink and a cold ham sandwich today," Godfrey answered.

They went through the line and paid for their purchases, then went out on the balcony overlooking the Tennessee River and sat down at one of the metal tables.

"This town has changed a lot since we were rookies." Godfrey said, unfolding the saran wrap on his ham sandwich and staring out at the river. He took a big bite, then exploded.

"Shit! This sandwich has *mayonnaise* on it."

"You've been makin' the same complaint for thirty years," Wallace observed. "Can't you ever learn that ham sandwiches in Knoxville, Tennessee *always* come with mayonnaise unless you ask for somethin' else on it?"

They sat in silence for a few minutes, munching sandwiches and sipping diet colas. "You're right, though," Godfrey said.

"About what?" Wallace asked.

"This town *has* changed a lot since we were rookies."

"Damn right! Did you hear about Whitey Brown?" Wallace asked, chewing with his mouth open.

"You mean the guy who used to be in forensics? Retired a couple of years before we did, right?"

"Yeah, that's the one. Well, a rookie KPD cop wrote him a speedin' ticket last week."

"Did he know Whitey was a retired cop?" Godfrey had finished his sandwich and was reaching for a cigarette, when he remembered that he had quit smoking three years earlier.

"If he didn't know before, he damn sure knew after I called him. You wanna know what he said to me?" Wallace didn't wait for a reply. "He said if I *ever* tried to influence him again in a criminal case that he'd go to the attorney general and file obstruction charges against me! Can you believe a rookie would talk that way to a man who was a cop when he was in diapers? They're like the fuckin' Hitler Youth, these days, Godfrey—no respect for them that paved the way for'em."

"Everything's changin'," Gordon. It ain't just rookie cops that treat us with disrespect. You remember Robert Pitt?"

"Yeah, yeah. I *told* you I remembered him. You been tryin' to talk about him all mornin'. He was one of the few nigger lawyers practicin' in this town when we was comin' up."

"Well, you remember how well me and him always got along, don't you?" Walt Godfrey said.

"You and old Pitt? Sure, I remember. You always called him *Cal*houn."

"Yeah! Me and him always got along *real* good. I'd call him Calhoun and he'd call me Officer Godfrey. Everybody got a kick out of it, even the judges. 'Cause Pitt couldn't deny that he was the spittin' image of that Algonquin Calhoun in the old *Amos n Andy* television show."

"You're right about that. They could've been twins. Except Pitt never talked that nigger talk. He was always so *proper*. Talked better than most white men. Somebody once told me he was a Rhodes Scholar, whatever that means."

"I always *thought* me and ol' Pitt was friends," Godfrey said. "I used to send him work, didn't I? Every time we busted a black whore or a pimp, I sent'em to Pitt. You might say, I gave him his start."

"So what makes you think that things has changed between you and Pitt?" Wallace asked.

"Well, I ran into him over at city court the other day. Hadn't seen him in three years. I walked right up, just like I'd done a thousand times in the last thirty years and said, 'How's it goin' there, *Cal*houn?'"

"He looked at me funny for a few seconds, then pulled up his chest and said to me, in a *real* smart tone of voice, 'My name is *Mister Pitt*, not *Calhoun*. I would appreciate it if you'd call me by my real name!' Then he just walked off without another word. I thought he was jokin' for a minute, but he didn't look back."

"You *sure* he wasn't pullin your leg?" Wallace asked.

"No, it wasn't a joke. He sounded downright nasty! Can you believe he talked to me like that after all the years me and him was friends?"

"Go figure," Wallace said, then belched loudly. "The world ain't like it used to be, is it?"

"No, it ain't. If ever there was a nigger that I expected *not* to put on airs, it was Robert Pitt. To be truthful, it sorta hurt my feelins', Gordon."

"I understand, Godfrey. God knows there's enough hate and bitterness without somebody like Robert Pitt bein' so insensitive and stirrin' up racial problems."

"Would you ask Pitt what set him off if you was me, Gordon?"

"*Hell, no!* You try to talk to him again and you're gonna get the same kind of crap that you get from all the other soul brothers. He's gonna try to tell you that you didn't treat *him* right, even when we all know you did. If it was me, I wouldn't ever speak to the black sonofabitch again. He's an ingrate. As far as I'm concerned, it's *Mister Pitt* who's got a problem, Godfrey—*not* you."

"I guess you're right, Gordon. All a man can do is treat everybody fair, includin' *mi-norities*. If *Mister* Pitt is ungrateful, it *is* his problem, not mine."

"Damn right!" Gordon Wallace said, then looked at his watch. "We better get movin' or we're gonna be late for court."

"Can't afford to be late, can we?" Godfrey asked. "People already think we're a couple of dinosaurs from another time who couldn't learn a new trick if we had to."

"Ain't that the truth," Wallace answered. "*Ain't* that the truth."

Death Watch

THE INTERCOM BESIDE the bed crackled and the old man's voice, querulous and reedy, sent rage rippling up John White's spine. Two or three times a week for thirty years, his father-in-law had been waking him up, usually for frivolous reasons.

In the early days of John's marriage to the old man's daughter, Big Mike Dawson had often roused him, ostensibly to talk business or have John drive him somewhere—usually downtown to pick up hookers. Of late, he had taken to demanding juice or a snack at least once a night—*anything* to make John's life miserable.

Cursing under his breath, John slipped on his robe and house shoes and walked down the hallway to his father-in-law's room. The light was on and the voluptuous, round-the-clock nurse was spraying nitroglycerine on the old man's tongue. She was well past her early youth, but still a good-looking woman.

"Calm down, Mr. Dawson," the nurse said. "What's wrong?"

"Deathwatch," the old man gasped, "I hear the deathwatch beetles! Can't you hear them? *There*, in the bedside table."

John stood staring at Big Mike Dawson's turkey gobbler neck and round bald head covered with those hideous age spots, as always repulsed by the sight. The nickname still lingered, though the old man had been reduced by time and stress almost to skin and bones. There was no color in his parchment-like skin and his bones showed through his face like those of a cadaver. Something had *really* scared the old coot. John felt a tingle of satisfaction.

"Don't just stand there, you damned idiot. *Listen*, John!"

John suppressed a retort as he had been doing for what seemed eternity but was really only a little over three decades, then put his ear close to the table beside the old man's bed. Sure enough, there was a distinct clicking noise.

"How odd," John said.

"No it's *not* odd," the old man snapped. "It's the deathwatch beetles!"

"Mr. Dawson," the nurse said in a tone of voice reserved for old people and children, "there's no such thing. You were just having a nightmare."

Her pale blond hair, streaked with silver and normally up in tight braids fell to her shoulders. Her gown was open and her breasts were exposed almost to the nipples under the thin gown she was wearing. John had a pang of lust as he looked at her. The old man had made it virtually impossible for him to see *any* woman since his wife's death three years earlier.

"Of course, there are deathwatch beetles, you *cow*! They lay their eggs in wood and the grubs eat it from the inside. My son-in-law would have known it if he ever listened to his betters." Big Mike had apparently realized that he had been seen in a moment of weakness. His way of recovering was exactly the same as his remedy for everything else he did, with blustering. A little color had come back into his lips.

"The old folks used to believe that death *always* followed the sound of deathwatch beetles. Of course, I never believed that crap myself. They're just plain old beetles, like powder-post beetles. They eat wood. It takes more than a few bugs to scare Big Mike Dawson."

"Sure, Mr. Dawson. *Nothing* scares you," John said. But he *had* been scared, terrified, in fact. It was the first time John had ever seen the old man show fear of *anything*.

"Mr. Dawson," the nurse said, as she straightened the old man's pillow, "you probably shouldn't go to work in the morning."

"Of course, I'll go to work in the morning! This so-called son-in-law never gave me any grandchildren. My poor daughter died of a broken heart because *he* was sterile as a mule. I keep hoping he'll finally learn something so I can pass on the business without worrying about it.

"Of course, with his heart in worse shape than mine, *you* might even get everything, Edith." The old man cackled, overcome by his own humor. Blue veins stood out in his head and tears of mirth came to his eyes.

John White flushed. He still couldn't help it, even after thirty cruel years of badgering. The old man knew perfectly well that it was his daughter who couldn't have children, but liked *his* version better.

When John had married Big Mike's daughter, it seemed a fair bet that his father-in-law wouldn't last long. Now, Big Mike was ninety-two and John was fifty-one, and had already undergone coronary bypass surgery. Sometimes he thought the old man stayed around for pure spite.

"We'll have none of that talk," the nurse began, "tomorrow...."

"You think maybe it's Isaac Silverman sent the deathwatch beetles, John? I outlived him didn't I? I had to wait fifty years, but I ended up with *everything* that old Jew owned." Once again, Big Mike chuckled at his own wit.

Competitors in the antique and estate sales business, Isaac Silverman and Big Mike Dawson had engaged in a grudge war that had begun when they were both callow youths. Finally, however, Big Mike Dawson—just two weeks earlier—had finally triumphed by default. His competitor had died. The bedside table with the beetles in it was a trophy, right out of Isaac Silverman's own bedroom.

"I don't know, Mr. Dawson. I didn't think you believed in ghosts," John said.

"I don't, you *damned idiot*; it was a joke! Get that table out of here and have it fumigated. And don't drag around all day tomorrow just because you lost a little sleep. I've always been able to work on no more than three hours a night. That's one reason I'm rich and you still run errands, *John Boy*."

John carried the small table out into the hall. He could still hear the old man complaining to the nurse about something or another. She had lasted for over a year; most of his nurses counted their time in weeks, or sometimes days.

Instead of going to bed, John went downstairs to the library and turned on the light. He poured himself a brandy, glancing at himself in the mirror. "I've still got my looks," he said to the mirror. "But they won't last forever." Indeed, he looked younger than his fifty-one years. He still had all his hair and it was a distinguished silver at the temples.

Turning to the shelves, he picked out the proper volume of the *Encyclopedia Britannica* and looked up "deathwatch beetle." It was an interesting article. The author said that there were 260 species, ranging from a tenth of an inch to half an inch in size, and that unlike some wood-eating beetles, the deathwatch had catholic tastes, infesting virtually every type of wood.

There was a picture of one of the creatures; it had a bell-shaped thorax and when viewed from the top, its head was hidden. According to the article, the larva of some species had been known to spend up to twenty or thirty years inside a piece of furniture before emerging as adults. The distinctive clicking sound, the article said, was caused by the larvae bumping their heads against the end of the tunnels they made while eating their way through the wood.

Best of all, they were the only thing that had *ever* scared Big Mike Dawson.

"Will you be riding in with us, Mr. White?" Carl, Big Mike's driver, asked.

"No, I'm going to check on a piece of furniture I saw at a roadside junk store."

"Make sure you don't dally around all morning," Big Mike said. "I might need some errands run today." The old man was dressed in his usual three-piece suit, and there was already egg yolk on one of the lapels, though it had just come from the cleaners. He ate four over-easy eggs every morning while John had oatmeal and bran muffins. Now past ninety, Big Mike often said he saw no reason to change his habits, despite an ever weakening heart. He viewed bran muffins and oatmeal as food for cattle and sissies, and never let John forget it.

"It won't take me long," John said.

"See that it doesn't. I'm ready to go, Carl." The big driver, light glistening from his ebony skin, helped the old man up and supported him to the door on wobbly legs. There was no reason for Mike Dawson to go to the office, except to make John White's life hell. The old man only sat sleeping and drooling on himself most of the day in his big, luxurious office, while his son-in-law ran the business from the same cramped cubicle he had been assigned his first day at work.

A few minutes later, John pulled his plain, but well-kept black Plymouth into a strip mall. He drove around for a minute before spotting what he was looking for. It was one of those electronic shops that advertised all sorts of gimmicks and gizmos in the Sunday paper.

Somewhat uneasily, as if entering a porno shop, John went in and walked over to the glass counter-top and looked at the array of strange objects. The cheerful, young man who seemed to be in charge was at the other end waiting on another customer. John had no idea what he was looking at. Finally, the clerk finished with his other customer and came over.

"How may I help you?" He was freckled and redheaded, a bright orange carrot color.

"I see your ads sometimes," John said, "about recording devices and that sort of thing."

"Want to bug somebody, do you? We've got all kinds of bugs; some of them are no bigger than a dime. I've got cameras small enough to fit inside a piece of jewelry All your snooping needs right here."

"Actually, I wanted something to send sound—you know, like as a joke to somebody who's in the bathroom, to make them think they're not alone," John said.

"I've got several transmitters, wireless or with wires, depending on what you want to spend. With a wireless transmitter there's no wire to tip anyone off, but batteries have to be replaced."

"Show me the wireless kind," John said. "Small ones."

THE OLD MAN's screams reached a high pitch, like a child in pain. John waited until he heard the nurse open Big Mike's bedroom door before he turned off the tape player that was transmitting the sound of deathwatch beetles to his father-in-law's headboard. John had recorded the sounds himself from the old bedside table before sending it out to be fumigated.

A moment later, John entered the old man's room; he had tousled his own hair and was feigning sleepiness. Big Mike Dawson was sitting up in bed, his face drained of color, gasping and wheezing. "The deathwatch beetles—I heard them again!"

"There are no deathwatch beetles, Mr. Dawson," the nurse said. "John took that table out of here last night."

"That's right," John said. "It's already been fumigated and you can have it back in a few days." He noticed that the old man's face had a blue tinge to it.

"I don't *care*. I heard them, just like last night. They're close to me. Listen!" The old man was suddenly wracked by a coughing spell. The nurse patted his back while John leaned over close to the bed.

"Mr. Dawson, I don't hear anything. Maybe it *really* was a nightmare this time," John said.

Rather than his usual rage, Big Mike's face showed relief. "Maybe it was," he said, then laid back down on the pillow.

After he had fallen asleep again, John and Edith stepped into the hall and stopped outside the old man's door. "He needs to go to the hospital," the nurse said. Once again, her robe was open and the view caused John catch his breath.

"He won't go." John said. "He's always refused. Every time we've gotten him there, it was after he passed out. That's why we have a nurse here at all times."

"Well, there's just so much I can do if he goes into cardiac arrest." She noticed that John was covertly staring at her breasts and didn't seem to be offended. Her hand fluttered near her robe, but she didn't close it.

"I know," John said. "He's old, though and set in his ways."

"I'm afraid that another attack like the one he just had may do him in. Goodnight."

The nurse was wrong. It took *two* more attacks to kill the old man. After the ambulance crew left with the body, John removed the tiny, high-tech transmitter that had been attached to the back of Big Mike Dawson's headboard and the micro-cassette recording of the death watch beetles and flushed them down his toilet.

EDITH CAME INTO the kitchen the next morning, wearing her robe, her hair still loose around her shoulders. It was the first time. Always before she had been dressed at breakfast. John wondered if she was still wearing the robe especially for him. There was definitely a lot of cleavage showing. She fixed herself a cup of coffee and took a seat at the table.

"It's sad," she said, shaking her head.

"Well, he lived a full life," John said, taking his last bite of oatmeal.

"I guess I'll need to be moving out," she said.

"Don't you like it here, Edith?"

"Well, yes but…"

"I have a bad heart too, remember? I take half a dozen pills every day and don't leave home without my little brown bottle."

"That's true," she said. "I guess I *did* forget. Mr. Dawson was a full-time job."

"That he was, but he's gone now. He even made his own funeral arrangements in advance. Any employee who doesn't show for his funeral tomorrow is to be fired. He was in control until the last." *Almost in control*, John thought.

"So, you want me to stay?" she asked.

"Of course. We can even renegotiate your benefits. Why don't we discuss it over lunch today. I'll pick you up around noon."

"All right." Her hand once more fluttered to her breasts where his gaze was fixed, but she made no move to deflect his view. They both looked up as Big Mike's driver opened the back door, wearing his jacket and drivers' cap.

"Mr. White, will you be needing me to drive you in today—or to the funeral home." The big man asked.

"No, that won't be necessary, Carl. I meant to talk to you this morning before I left. I won't be needing a driver any longer. I can probably arrange a job for you at the warehouse, if you'd like. If not, I'll have the bookkeeper write you a check for a month's severance pay. Take a couple of days and think it over."

"Thank you, sir." Carl walked over and laid the keys to the Lincoln on the table. "Just have the bookkeeper write me a check. I haven't been back to Alabama in a long time. It's time I took a trip home."

"If that's what you want," said John White, captain of his own fate for the first time in more than thirty years. It was a heady feeling. "I'll see you at lunch, Edith." He wasn't sure, but he thought Edith winked ever so slightly.

It was a glorious ride to the office that morning. Big Mike's Lincoln was a nice, comfortable car, but there was a red Mercedes that John had been looking at with longing at a dealership near the offices of "Big Mike's Elegant Antiques." Now he could have it. He could have *anything* he wanted because the company was his, lock stock and barrel. He knew it was because the will, or the threat of changing the will, had been used as by Big Mike as a cudgel to keep John in line.

He was whistling as he entered the office at the huge antique shop, *his* antique shop. The receptionist looked up, startled, as he entered the lobby. "I've been telling everyone you wouldn't be in today," she said.

"Well, you were wrong. Isn't this what Big Mike would have wanted—business as usual?"

"I suppose so." She dropped her eyes.

"Find the number for that Mercedes dealership a couple of blocks down the street and get the manager on the line. Also, call Steve from the warehouse. I need to see him in my office—Big Mike's old office."

Inside the office, walking on the plush, red carpet, the total reality hit him for the first time. *He was free!* His heart began to pound so hard that his breathing became labored. He fished out the little brown bottle and put a nitro tablet under his tongue; the tightness in his chest went away just as the knock came at the door.

"Come in," he said.

Steve Aldridge, the warehouse foreman came in, hat in hand, looking uneasy. "You wanted to see me?"

"Yes, Steve. How long have you been with the company?"

"Twenty-two years." The man swallowed hard.

"It's about time you got promoted. Make somebody else warehouse foreman. You're going to take over my slot as the new Director of Acquisitions. After all, you know as much about antiques as I do. You can have my old desk—until I find suitable rental space, then you can have your own office."

"Thank you, sir." He seemed immensely relieved.

"I'll decide on an appropriate raise when I have time. But there's something else I want you to do for me today."

"Whatever you need, Mr. White."

"You can call me John, just like always, Carl. I'm not like my former father-in-law.'"

"All right…. John."

"I want you to measure this desk, then go down to the warehouse and find a *bigger* one. If there isn't a bigger one there, find one somewhere else. Move it up here as soon as possible."

"That's a pretty big desk, John."

"I don't care if it's only an *inch* wider, just so it's bigger. We'll match the rest of the new furniture to the desk. Do you have me covered?"

"It'll be here when you get back," Steve said.

As the former warehouse foreman left, the receptionist buzzed him. "I have the Mercedes dealership on the line."

"Thanks, Shelly. By the way, hire a new receptionist and order three computers. You're going to be my full-time secretary. Oh, and order cell phones for me and Steve."

"Yes sir, I'm transferring the call to you." She sounded bewildered.

There hadn't been a new piece of equipment in the office since she arrived. Big Mike hadn't liked newfangled gadgets.

He held the phone, waiting for the click; when it came, he said, "This is John White, owner of Big Mikes Elegant Antiques. You have a red Mercedes in your showroom. I need you start the paperwork. I'll be down to pick it up in a few minutes."

God it felt good to give orders!

IT WAS NEARLY six when John got back to the office. He was a little tipsy from the wine at lunch and the drinks that he and Edith had shared afterwards. She was a lively woman, much livelier than he had suspected.

She had clapped her hands together when she saw the red Mercedes. They had made plans to spend a quiet evening at home, watching a movie on the DVD player he had sent her out to buy. It would be like having a wife again—except he could fire her whenever he wanted.

He met Shelly, the receptionist, at the door. She seemed startled again. "I was just about to lock up. But I can stay, if you need me."

"There'll be none of *that* from now on," John said jovially. "By the way, are you still driving that old, yellow Toyota?"

"Yes," she lowered her eyes, "I wish I could afford something better, but…"

"You know that black Plymouth of mine?"

"Yes, sir."

"Well, it's yours now. Have somebody from the warehouse pick it up tomorrow. It's not much, but it's only two years old. I'll sign it over to you."

"I don't know what to say," she said.

"Say goodbye. You've been a good employee. There'll be a raise with your new title." She started to say something else, but tears filled her eyes and she left hurriedly.

"Be loyal to your employees," he said to the air, "and they'll be loyal to you." Mike Dawson, the greedy old bastard, had never learned that. He was too damned stingy to give anyone a break. But things would be different now. Hell, they were *already* different.

John opened the door to his office and turned on the light. It was already growing dark outside. He had forgotten about ordering the new desk. It was magnificent—and definitely bigger than the other one. He walked around and plopped down on the soft leather of the chair from which Big Mike had ruled his empire. Life was good.

He closed his eyes and smiled. It took a moment before he heard the faint sound. *Click. Click. Click. Click. Click.* He couldn't tell where the sound was coming from.

John's eyes opened and his heart began to pound as he looked around for an explanation. He got up and went to the door and looked out. The outer office and showroom were empty and there was only silence.

"Just my imagination playing tricks," he said aloud. "After all, *good* stress is as hard on the system as bad stress." That's what his cardiologist had told him. And he had definitely been through a fantastic day. He sat back down, leaned back and smiled to himself.

Click. Click. Click. Click. Click.

He recoiled from the desk as if from a poisonous viper. *Deathwatch beetles*.! But, no. That was silly. In twenty-five years he had encountered them only once. What were the odds that he would run across them twice in three days? It was ridiculous. He was tired, tipsy and his imagination was running wild. He willed himself not to hear the sound anymore.

Click. Click. Click. Click. Click.

Suddenly John realized that he was soaked in sweat. That was a *bad* sign. He was also breathing rapidly and shallowly. He fought for control, but his heart raced away and a burning sensation began to spread from just under his breastbone out his right arm.

Then, it was as if an elephant had sat on his chest, just as he had heard the sensation described. He pulled the nitroglycerine bottle from his pocket and put one under his tongue, but it didn't relieve the pain. He fumbled for another, then dropped the bottle, spilling the tiny pills across the bright red carpet.

He started for the door to yell for Carl, then remembered that he had fired the driver that morning. Staggering back to the desk, he grabbed the phone and clumsily punched in 911, but by the time an operator answered, he couldn't focus anymore. His brain wasn't getting enough oxygen and the pain was too intense.

It sounded to the operator as if he had gasped, "*Death watch.*"

The 911 system had locked on his telephone number and address, so fire department paramedics broke down the office door in less than ten minutes. But for John White, they were seven minutes too late.

When they found him, he had an undissolved nitroglycerine tablet stuck to his lower lip and the rest were still scattered on the floor.

"SO, YOU THINK you can run the company?" The lawyer asked. He was a lean man of forty with a crew cut and the intensity of a cat on the stalk, who played handball almost every night.

"Sure. But what's going to happen to all of us?" Steve, the ex-warehouse foreman and now manager of Big Mike's Elegant Antiques, asked.

"Nothing for the time being. In the event that no heirs were named, my firm was designated as executor. With John dead, there *are* no heirs. We don't have to be in any hurry. I'm sure we can find a buyer who will retain all employees. Maybe we can even work something out so you guys can buy the company for yourselves."

"That sounds good," Steve Eldridge said. "It's really sad, though. John was a good guy."

"Yeah, he was," the lawyer said. "Nothing like his bastard father-in-law. Sometimes it seems that the good guys can't win."

"He was on the floor when the fireman got here. I wonder if he ever got to sit at his new desk," Steve said.

"That's a fine-looking piece of furniture," the lawyer said, running his hand over the surface. "Nobody makes them like this any more."

"Yeah, it's the only desk in the warehouse bigger than the one that was already in here. It came from the Isaac Silverman sale—Big Mike's archenemy—a couple of weeks ago. "

Daddy Hated Kudzu

I WATCHED FROM my picture window as my half-brother pulled himself laboriously from the front seat of a red Cadillac. Tommy has always been a Cadillac person, obvious and ostentatious. The Cadillac he was driving when last I saw him was yellow. He appeared to have put on another ten pounds, but otherwise looked pretty much the same—self-absorbed, humorless and troubled.

Tommy and I had drifted apart through the years. He had been no more interested in farming than I, but neither did the scholar's life appeal to him. After two years of college, he dropped out, went into the business of building houses and prospered at it. I went away to school and never really left the halls of academia again.

Even my token trips home stopped two years ago. I went to Tennessee on holidays while my father was alive, and occasionally for a short time after his death while Aunt Clovia still lived in the old house. I had not been back at all since she died. There had not been even a letter between us—not until yesterday.

Two years older than me, he has grown into a morbidly obese man with a flushed face who will probably be dead before sixty, the victim of too much red meat and too many cigarettes. We parted amicably enough the last time, mostly because Tommy had finally gotten what he wanted, which was agreement from me to subdivide Daddy's farm, where we both grew up, and build houses.

He had brought it up the first time right after our father's funeral, but I refused to sign the papers. "Aunt Clovia has been like a mother to us," I argued. "It's her home and I'm not going to move her out."

"I don't want to put her in the street! We'll get her a nice apartment and see that she has what she needs. But the market's good right now and I need to strike while the iron's hot."

When I still refused, there were harsh words. He did not, however, broach the subject again—not until after Aunt Clovia's funeral seven months later. I signed an agreement then, giving Tommy the right to do as he wished with the property, paying little attention to the details because real money has little more meaning for me than the kind you use with a Monopoly board.

Our lack of communication was why his call yesterday had come as a surprise. His message was even more puzzling. Tommy was never any good at keeping a secret *or* telling a lie. He had simply informed me that he would be at my place today to discuss something important.

I smiled to myself as he puffed his way up my walk, in a hurry. He was always like Daddy in that respect, though they weren't really related by blood—always on some unwritten schedule. I have not been around Tommy enough to know what type of goad he uses to push himself to the limit. With Daddy, there was never any doubt.

Daddy hated kudzu.

He hated kudzu more than he hated preachers and religion. I never knew where he acquired his hatred of preachers and religion, but he hated kudzu because it was an interloper, a thing which did not belong in East Tennessee.

Among my earliest memories are of my father hacking away at the twisted vines that seemed to snake up around his ankles, even as he was destroying them. When the ground was devoid of the plant he would spread herbicides, like Hannibal sowing salt on the ground where Carthage once stood.

"Damned foreign weed," he would growl, old felt hat in hand, pausing to wipe away the sweat from his seamed forehead, where the tan of his face met the fish-belly white of his scalp. "And damn them who brought this curse in on us."

My daddy always seemed old to me, even when I was little. He was in his forties when he married my momma, a confirmed bachelor until he first saw her. She was fifteen and pregnant at the time with Tommy—by a hired hand who stopped in the fall of 1946 to help with my grandfather's wheat harvest and planted a seed of his own before leaving.

Daddy was a one-woman man, never in love until he met my momma, never in love again. She *was* an extraordinary beauty, with cornsilk blonde hair and eyes as green as spring clover. Daddy took her in and married her after her father had turned her out of the house for disgracing the family.

Not only did he marry her, but he sold his farm in Claiborne County and moved to Union County so that she would not have to be reminded of her indiscretion every day. He was the first member of the Justice family to ever voluntarily leave Claiborne County. That was how much he loved Momma. He never showed a difference between me and Tommy and never mentioned the past. His love blinded him to everything that had gone before.

The only time I ever saw anything set Daddy into a rage—except when he got started on kudzu or preachers—was an offhand, snickering comment made by one of his numerous cousins at a Justice family gathering, speculating about Tommy's *real* father.

Daddy whipped him soundly, in front of the entire Justice clan, the unfortunate man's blood spraying in the air around him every time my father's veined fist connected with a sound like you get from a ripe melon when you drop it on concrete.

"He's as *real* a son as a man ever had," Daddy said, as the rest of his clan looked on in open-mouthed awe, "and *anybody* who says different, will answer to me. I don't care if it's the Devil himself."

That subject never came up again at a Justice family gathering, on the one trip a year that we made at Christmas. Aunt Clovia who moved in after Momma left, said that God was punishing our father for the sin of idolatry, for loving our mother more than a man ought to love anything in this world. Aunt Clovia was a staunch Primitive Baptist, like all the Justices except my father, but she never voiced her opinions to him, not about religion *or* idolatry.

The farm Daddy bought in Union County was not nearly as good as the one left behind. It had lain fallow for fifteen years, tied up in court because of a family dispute. The kudzu had all but taken over by the time Daddy moved Momma into the old ramshackle frame house.

Kudzu is a hardy plant, a survivor, admirable in its own way. It's a legume, a member of the same family as the common bean, and native to China and Japan. It arrived here by way of the Philippines, first brought in to halt soil erosion in Alabama. That it did admirably, then proceeded to spread its tentacles across the Southeastern United

States and points beyond, dropping water-sucking roots every few feet—which is the reason for its hardiness.

Visitors from up north sometimes mistake it for ivy when they see it in the places where it has crept up and covered telephone poles and lines, or totally buried trees in its path. It *does* look sort of like a giant ivy in the summer. In the winter you see it only as a tangle of dead vines.

These things I learned about kudzu when I was studying agriculture, before I switched my major to English literature. Daddy never saw *any* virtue in the kudzu, though. He made it his enemy, a relentless enemy, which had to be constantly attacked and ripped up from the ground. He would wade in, swinging that briar scythe like a rural Saint George in bibbed overalls, determined to hack off the head of the dragon.

As soon as Tommy and I were old enough, we were recruited for the crusade. "*This*," my father would snarl, waving his arms over the fields of kudzu, "is what happens when man tampers with nature. "This filthy weed don't belong here. May them who brought it in on us burn in hell—if there is a hell."

By the time I was eight years old, daddy had whipped all the kudzu on our farm, except for about a half acre of it on a hill about two hundred yards from the house. He left it for last because no crops would be grown there; that was the spot where he intended to build Momma's dream house. It was to have been built exactly the way Momma wanted it—white clapboard, trimmed in red, with a swing on the front porch.

Momma would clap her hands and laugh like a child when Daddy talked about the house. At such times, it was easy to remember that she was closer to her sons' age than to her husband's. That deep musical laughter, bubbling out like a spring of crystal water is what I remember most clearly about Momma. She would shake that great mane of golden hair into waves as she tossed her head back to laugh.

The house was never built, of course. We had just begun to attack the kudzu at the bottom of that last hill when the Bible salesman arrived and turned our lives up-side-down.

It was early on a Monday morning, just before school, when Cleveland Keck pulled that yellow and white Nash Rambler up to the house. He was a tall, gangling man, just about Momma's age. His blond hair was curly and worn longer than most men wore it in those days of crew cuts and barber shops where you had to take a number on weekends. Daddy would later mutter under his breath to Tommy and me that long hair on a man was a sin. That puzzled me a little, considering Daddy's scorn for religion in general.

That Bible salesman was a charmer, and he had Momma under his spell from the beginning. His suit was of a loud, reddish brown color, a cheap cotton blend, but it looked fancy to us. His shoes were two-tone oxfords, which he kept polished to a high gloss. He wore nylon socks to match his ties. The first day I saw him they were both a garish yellow and black pattern. To a couple of country kids and their momma who had been no further away than Knoxville, he looked like a man of the world.

"Howdy," he said, showing his teeth in the way of wolves and salesmen of all stripes. He tipped his white straw hat with the black band. "Name is Cleveland Keck, Ma'am. I'm from the New Jerusalem Bible Company of Culver's Junction, Mississippi. I understand that you have a room to rent. I wonder if I might speak to your mother?"

"I'm the mother of this here house," Momma said, dimpling up. She pushed a strand of her blonde hair from off her forehead. "We got a room for rent, but my husband don't take kindly to preachers or religion."

"Well, ma'am. I just *sell* Bibles—don't preach out of 'em. Surely your husband won't object to a man earnin' a livin' the only way he knows how. Sellin' Bibles is no different than sellin' brushes."

"I reckon you're right, but he don't care much for strangers either," Momma replied.

"If a'body was from *around* here, I guess he'd already have a place to stay, wouldn't he? I'd not be much trouble and I'll be on my way in a few weeks."

"I'll talk to my husband," Momma told him, "but he'll have the final word. And what was your name, again?"

"Grover Cleveland Keck at your service, Ma'am." He swept that hat off his head like a cavalier. I could tell that Momma was as impressed as we were. "You can call me Cleve."

"Come back about five o'clock, Mr. Keck, and I'll let you know then. Rent's eight dollars a week and you'd take supper with us. The room is over the barn, but it's real nice. "

Daddy was dead set against the Bible salesman, of course, just as he had been dead set against building the apartment in the loft over the barn in the first place, but he hardly ever said no to Momma when she really wanted something. He gave a token resistance, but when she pointed out that the money could go towards furnishings for her dream house, he caved in and went to wash up for supper, muttering under his breath.

Cleveland Keck arrived right on time that night. Daddy reluctantly shook hands with him, but had nothing to say. Tommy and I carried his two suitcases up to the room over the barn and he carried his metal sample case. We never saw him arrive or depart without that case. He carried it like a talisman wherever he went.

Supper was a lighthearted affair for everyone but Daddy that first night. The Bible salesman kept Momma laughing and clapping her hands all through supper with bits of gossip about the Governor of Tennessee and his family—which purportedly came from firsthand knowledge. To us, Nashville was as far away as Cairo, Egypt, and it was just as glamorous.

After sopping up the last of the bean juice with his cornbread, Daddy got up and pushed his chair back. "Come on, boys. We got some kudzu to kill. A farmer ain't got time to sit around and lollygag in the evenin's like *some* people does."

We both followed him that night with exaggerated sighs, leaving Cleveland Keck and Momma still laughing and cutting up. By that time, the kudzu had been eliminated to a point about fifty yards or so up the hill towards the crest where Momma's dream house was supposed to be built. We worked every night except Sundays on the kudzu eradication. Though Daddy didn't go to church himself, he took note of the sensibilities of his Baptist and Pentecostal neighbors.

Tommy and I both wanted to sit and listen to Cleveland Keck, Bible salesman and world traveler, but it was not to be, except for the brief minutes which Daddy allowed himself for supper every night. Then it was out to the hill for combat with the hateful Asian vine.

In fact, Daddy's time at the supper table grew shorter after the Bible salesman came. It hurt him, I think, to watch as a stranger evoked in his wife a sort of magical laughter which he had never been able to coax forth. She would sit, chin in hand, green eyes wide, absorbing everything that the tall, lanky salesman said.

I guess Daddy saw the problem coming but didn't know what to do. The salesman had been there a month before *I* found out what was going on and I didn't tell anybody, not even Tommy. At the age of eight, I knew that what I saw was wrong, but my mind could not grasp the horrible implications of what my momma was doing.

My Donald Duck lunch box had been left on the porch that morning and I had dashed back down the driveway to retrieve it. As I got to the yard, I saw Momma step into the barn and close the door behind her. At first, I thought she was gathering eggs. Then I realized that she was still in her old terry-cloth housecoat. She never left the house until she was fully dressed, even when Daddy was working the other side of the farm and not apt to come home before dinner, as he was that day.

I moved on tiptoes towards the barn. Even though I didn't understand the full implications, I knew a secret when I saw one. Slipping around to the back, I climbed the ladder leading to the window. Before Daddy built the apartment, the ladder had given access to the loft from outside. It had been left though it no longer had any use.

Holding my breath that morning, I eased my eyes up over the wooden window frame. My heart pounded as I focused on that dim room. My mother was in the process of letting the robe slide away from her shoulders to puddle on the linoleum floor. I had never seen a naked female before, but there stood my mother in all her glory, trembling as she approached the bed and the extended arms of Cleveland Keck, seller of Bibles from the New Jerusalem Publishing Company.

That memory is now more than fifty years old, but still as vivid as the day I was witness to it. My mother, at that moment, became the essence of every woman who had ever lived. It was imprinted like a baby duck as the vision burned into my mind. It was a magical fragment of eternity, so far divorced from the everyday world that time itself ceased to exist.

It was the school bus, grinding gears down the side of the ridge, that broke the spell. I dropped lightly to the ground, picked up my lunch box and ran on rubber-soled, black high-top sneakers to the road. I was possessed of a secret never revealed until this moment, a secret between me and my mother—one which she was not even aware of having shared.

Soon after the barn incident, my parents began to argue, quietly at first, in the privacy of their bedroom. Within days, however, the arguments grew too loud and fierce to hide behind closed doors. Daddy wanted the Bible salesman gone. Momma steadfastly refused, insisting that we needed the money. Mr. Keck, the object of the arguments, never let on, though we all knew he *had* to have heard them.

Every evening Cleveland Keck pulled into the driveway in his little Nash Rambler and got out carrying the metal case in which he kept his wares. It would rest on the floor during supper and went to his room with him when he retired. He would sit down, as if nothing were wrong, and regale us with tales of faraway places like Birmingham and even New York City. Daddy would eat without speaking, tell the two of us to follow him, then stomp out to attack the kudzu with fresh vengeance.

It was three months after the Bible salesman's arrival when the situation came to a head. Tommy and I had arrived from school and instead of being greeted by the smell of bubbling pinto beans and ham hocks, we found Momma packing her old plaid suitcase.

"Are we goin' somewhere, Momma?" My heart was pounding because I sensed that something was not right, that my world was in jeopardy.

"I...Mr. Keck is givin' me a ride to Atlanta," she said, not looking at us as she folded her tattered and mended underwear in the suitcase.

"What about *us?*" I asked, swallowing hard.

"When I'm settled, I'll come back after you and Tommy. I love both of you, but I have to go. I just *have* to."

"Don't you love Daddy anymore," I asked.

"It's not that, Jimmy. Your daddy's a good man, but he's old enough to be *my* daddy. I'm smotherin'. I don't expect you to understand now, but some day you will."

The argument was fierce and loud when Daddy came home from the fields and found Momma waiting with the packed suitcase. Looking back through the years, I realized just how much my mother was to be admired for waiting to tell Daddy what she was going to do. It would have been easier for her to have simply sneaked away one afternoon, leaving him a note. Momma had grit, though. She did not take the easy way.

After two hours or so, Daddy opened the door from their bedroom and came out. His eyes were filled with tears and his voice was strangely hoarse. It was the first and last time I ever saw him cry. We could see Momma sitting on the bed behind him, her face also streaked with tears.

"Boys," he said, "you two go on to bed. Me and your momma still has things to discuss and you shouldn't have to hear it."

Neither of us mentioned that we had not been fed or that it was barely dark. We crept upstairs, glad to be away from the argument. As we climbed in bed, we heard the Nash Rambler putter into the yard. It was the last time. When we got up, our mother and all her personal possessions were gone, along with the Bible salesman and his car. We never saw either of them again.

Daddy sat on the bed all of the next day in his and Momma's room, staring at the wall, leaving the room only long enough to milk the cow. It was the first day, except for Sundays, either of us had ever seen him stay away from the fields when crops were waiting to be worked. The second day he drove his old pickup truck into Knoxville and brought his widowed and childless sister, Clovia, to live in his house and raise his sons.

Life for us fell into a new pattern the first night Aunt Clovia was there. Daddy went out to work the fields at daylight, as usual. That evening, though, he ate supper, then went out on the porch and sat in the swing until bed time. It was a frightening change for Tommy and me. Our momma had left and our daddy was violating the laws of our known universe. The third night, Tommy got up from the supper table and walked to the door. He hitched up his blue-jeans.

"Daddy, are we gonna get after that damned, stinkin' kudzu? It'll take back the hill if we don't stay with it."

"No, we ain't gonna kill kudzu no more," Daddy said in a tired and defeated voice, not even bothering to correct Tommy's use of a profanity. "Let the filthy, foreign vine have that hill. We'll mow the grass right up to the edge, but that hill is forsaken, just like me.

"Let the kudzu have it, and every time we look at it let's remember that women are treacherous and deceitful. Maybe you boys can be spared what I've been through."

And so it was. We farmed and kept the land clear, but the hill where Momma's dream house was to have been built, once more became a thick carpet of twisted kudzu vines. Every night, Daddy sat on that porch, staring at the hill. In the end, as his death neared, Aunt Clovia told us that in later years he would often talk to Momma, as if she could hear him from across the years, from wherever she had fled.

Daddy went on farming until he was 80 years old, long after I began to teach English and Tommy began to build houses. Daddy's warning about women apparently sunk in. Neither Tommy nor I ever married. I went out with a lot of women through the years—mostly slender blonde women with green eyes—but marriage never crossed my mind.

"Come in, Tommy. You're looking good," I lied to him as he stood on my porch.

"For a fat man with high blood pressure, I guess I'm good." He walked through my front door and put down a large, plastic garbage bag. "Can you spread out some newspaper, Jimmy?" Always a man of action and few words. Right to the point.

"Sure," I answered, picking up my evening *Herald*. "You've got my curiosity piqued," I smiled with a question in my eyes. "Have you struck oil on the farm?"

He watched me spread the paper, which I had not read, over my white carpet.

"Not hardly," Tommy answered, missing the irony as usual. He turned the bag up and dumped it unceremoniously on the newspaper. The room was suddenly filled with a moldy odor. The object on the paper was blackened with age and soil, but I instantly recognized Cleveland Keck's sample case, even after forty years. I looked at Tommy, another question in my eyes.

"No," he said. "Just the sample case with a few moldy leather and paper scraps inside. Backhoe pulled the case up almost as soon as we started digging on the side of that hill. He waited for me to speak but I just stared at the Cleveland Keck's sample case.

"They *are* out there, though. You *know* that, don't you? Momma and Cleveland Keck are buried on that hill somewhere. That's why we never heard from her again. Daddy killed both of them and buried them up there in the kudzu."

"The Bible salesman's car…"

"My guess," Tommy said, answering my question before I could get it out, "is that it's in a hundred feet of water in one of the limestone quarries scattered all over Union and Knox County. Daddy had all night to do what he did."

"Are you going to…"

"No." He has always answered my unasked questions, sometimes to my annoyance. "I've shut the operation down. I'm going to let sleeping dogs lie. I don't want the money enough to open that can of worms while we're still around to be embarrassed. Maybe my children or yours— if we ever have any—can develop that subdivision."

"It's ironic, isn't it?"

"What's ironic?" Tommy asked, wrinkles forming on his high forehead.

"Daddy loved Momma as much as he hated kudzu and preachers, but kudzu was the only memorial he could give her without attracting attention."

Tommy stared at me for a moment, a little puzzled, I suppose, as the irony passed over his practical and much-too-literal head.

The Pretend Family Next Door

THE PRETEND FAMILY used to go out and play on almost every warm, sunny day. There was a pretend mother, a pretend father and three pretend children. The father was an engineer and captain in the Army Reserves, the mother a certified public accountant. They pretended to play because the mother thought it was what families ought to do. In fact, everything they pretended to be and do was based on the mother's perception of how things *ought* to be.

Their real name was Pate and the mother and father pretended that they really enjoyed the games of kick ball or rolly-bat in their immaculately manicured backyard. When the children were small, they protested having to participate, but as they grew older, each of them bowed to the inevitable and also learned to pretend.

Captain Pate, as his wife called him, was a thin, short, wiry man with lacquered-down blond hair, a round face with perpetually puckered lips and a pale, colorless little toothbrush of a mustache. His dark eyes, contrasting with his pale complexion, always seemed to glitter like the eyes of a rodent caught in the headlights of a car, and his nervous disposition kept his face twitching almost constantly—as if the mustache was constantly ticking his pointed nose.

Mrs. Pate was a lump of a woman, shapeless and doughy, even when she was dieting—which was most of the time—with a pale mottled complexion, features that appeared not to have been done in much detail, and a square head. Sometimes she would boast about losing thirty pounds, but you never could tell the difference. Her stubby arms and seemingly ankleless legs, resembling those of an elephant, hippopotamus or rhinoceros, condemned her to a life sentence of looking squat, even when she had very little body fat.

The children had inherited the worst traits of both parents. They got her squatness and short limbs and his nervous energy and pointed face. During their pretend games, they would jerkily dart about the yard, reminding me of the little toy robots on rollers that came out in the fifties. None of them could catch, kick, or throw the ball with any skill. They were the clumsiest human beings I had ever seen.

"Stair-step children" was what Mrs. Pate called them—two years apart, methodically planned that way because that's what the experts said was best. Mrs. Pate was big on what the experts said, though she never quoted sources. An abortion had been required in order maintain the correct age ratio, or she had told me.

My wife once speculated what sex between them was probably like: "Can't you just *see* it," Linda giggled. "That puny little man perched on top of her, trying to keep his balance, his little mousy nose twitching, and her yelling out in that opera singer voice, '*Yes, Captain. Yes, yes, yes!*' Or, '*Oh random chance, oh random chance!*'—she being an atheist, and all."

I preferred not to think about that particular vision.

When we first moved in next door they only had one child. Neither of them had a job at that time. He was working on his master's degree in engineering and earning a little money as a weekend warrior. She was staying home because the experts said it was bad for children to be separated from their mother at an early age.

All of us within hearing range doubted the wisdom of her words because we often heard her screaming in frustration at her less-than-perfect children. Her tirades increased in decibels and duration through the years with the birth of each child. We couldn't help but hear because they kept their windows open to save on electricity during the summer—in a split-foyer house designed for central heat and air conditioning—not window fans.

Apparently Mrs. Pate didn't realize that her high, falsetto voice echoed all over the hilly neighborhood. It was a warbling, piercing voice that made me shudder every time she spoke or shouted.

She would ambush me as I went to the mailbox in the afternoon. I guess she needed to talk to an adult once in a while; and it was my penance, it seemed, for some earlier forgotten sin, to fulfill that mission. No matter how carefully I planned my trip out to the road, and no matter how I rushed, she almost always managed to come out the door in time to intercept me.

Sometimes she talked about the weather or a crime that had

occurred in the neighborhood. But any subject would do: "That's a new car isn't it, Ray?" she warbled out one day, just before I was able to get back inside my house. She demanded to be called "Mrs. Pate," by *everyone*, but always first names when talking to others.

"Yes it is," I replied, trying to be pleasant.

"I wish *we* could afford a new car," she said wistfully. "I guess *some* people just have all the luck. We'd be living in a shack now if our parents hadn't given us the down payment on this house as a wedding gift."

My jaws ached as I restrained myself from telling her that luck had little to do with it, and if she would get off her lazy ass and get a job, she could have almost anything she wanted.

It seemed unfair to her, I'm sure, that two people like my wife and me, with less than three years of college between us, should be living the good life while two talented and highly educated people like her and her husband had to scrimp through, driving junk cars that billowed smoke. She never said it outright, but I always understood what she meant.

We hadn't been living in our house long when the captain came up to the fence one evening as I was washing my police cruiser. "Could I speak to you, Mr. Wolfe."

"Sure." I put down my sponge and walked over to the chain-link fence.

"I'm afraid we have a *very* serious problem," he said, nose twitching above his little mustache and puckered lips. For a moment I was afraid he was going to tell me that one of my boys had been peeking in his windows or molesting his daughter.

"What would that be, Mr. Pate?"

"*This.*" He bent down and pointed to a small Maple sapling, just a seedling really, that had sprung up on my side, almost touching of his side of the fence. "That can do some real damage over time."

When I reached down and yanked it up by the roots, he seemed startled at my hastiness and what I told him. "Put this in your compost heap and feel free to deal with any further such problems in the future, Mr. Pate."

"Thank you," he said. "But I'd *never* bother anyone else's plants. I know how important a person's lawn is." He pointedly glanced at my yard as he made the statement. I've always kept it mowed, but never been a fanatic about it. The Pate yard was a lush, green carpet with flowers set in neat, almost mathematical little plots, even after the children were big enough to play outside. They knew better than to touch the flowers. It was obvious that the captain didn't approve of my haphazard yard work.

I don't think he really approved of the police car parked in my driveway, either. But he never said anything about it, even when I sometimes turned on the blue-lights and siren at the urging of my own boys or other neighborhood children. There was always the feeling that Mr. Pate considered me—and my sons—to be roughnecks.

My sons were not allowed in his yard because I *knew* they would trample the flowers. Once, when my oldest son was playing with a balsa wood airplane, it landed on the Pate roof and Captain Pate told him it had knocked a tile loose. The very idea that an ounce of balsa wood had damaged the roof was absurd. I guess that's why the nervous engineer never did mention it to me.

For years, the pretend children were allowed to come into my yard on occasion, but their father would hover near the fence, listening for naughty words from the raucous boys, and making certain that my roughnecks didn't bully his model sons or talk dirty before his daughter. It was the issue of children that finally freed me from having to talk to him at all.

The elder of the two pretend sons was sly and mean from birth. You could see it in his glittering, little eyes. He never missed an opportunity to hurl a rock at a dog or bird, or to ram smaller children with his bicycle. He inflicted pain every chance he got on a pet or smaller child—including his own brother and sister.

One afternoon the little sadist went too far and my middle son, who was the same age, bloodied his nose. Mr. Pate—after checking to see if my cruiser was there, I'm sure—stormed over and gave my wife a lecture on civilized behavior and child-rearing. She laughed in his face, unable to ignore his pompous intensity. When I came home I went over and explained that we were quite competent to raise our own children and that he could keep his little monster at home if he was worried about him.

His "revenge" was to stop speaking and to forbid his children to come into our yard. Hope soared for a few hours that Mrs. Pate would also shun me, but she didn't. The very next day she waylaid me between the porch and the mailbox to tell me that her husband had been dropped from the active reserve roster due to military budgets cuts, and that she would be taking a few accounting jobs to make ends meet. She wanted to know who did our taxes.

Needless to say, I told her that we were happy with our current accountant. The last thing I needed was for *her* to know my business.

I never had another conversation with Captain Pate, though I still had to endure his wife's piercing, falsetto voice during trips to the mailbox. She kept me updated, so I knew when her husband finally got his masters degree and went to work. It was a job well below his education and skills, she told me—a draftsman's position really.

"It's a shame," she said in her annoying voice, "that a man who did everything by the book, who worked hard for his degree, can't find a good job. Why, garbage men make more money than he does!" She glanced at my cruiser, but didn't say anything about the income level of police officers, though I knew she thought it was much higher than it really was.

By the time their eldest child was twelve, the Pates were driving better cars, but always used ones. For a while it seemed they were actually beginning to prosper. She took a full-time accounting job, which paid well. He acquired and lost three positions in drafting rooms and his wife continued to lament the waste of his talents. It all seemed clear to me, though. I couldn't imagine being locked in a room with his nervous twitching for eight hours at a time, or that anyone would ever trust him with *any* responsibility.

I guess it was his last engineering failure that did it. One morning as I was getting the newspaper, I saw him climb into his old Ford. He was wearing a uniform from a fast food place and when he saw that I was watching, he quickly turned away and dropped his head. In his eyes, working as a lowly, unskilled burger flipper—or even as the manager of such a place—must have seemed the final blow.

One year, when he was out of work more than usual, I had offered to put in a good word at the sheriff's department to get him a part-time summer job, and he had haughtily informed that it hardly seemed proper employment for an engineer. I didn't say anything about beggars being choosy—though I thought it.

It was early one Saturday afternoon when I was working first shift that I heard a cruiser being dispatched to the pretend family's house. Only mildly interested, I headed in that direction. I figured that Mrs. Pate had called the sheriff's department, as she had done so many times before, because one of our neighbors was burning weeds, or because a neighborhood child was practicing a musical instrument too loudly while her children were taking their mandatory afternoon nap.

When the responding officer, in a shaky voice, called for a supervisor, a homicide detective and the medical examiner a few minutes later, I sped up.

When I got there, Bob Rawlston, a rookie patrol officer under my command, was standing on the front porch taking deep breaths, obviously rattled. The homicide detective on duty, Happy Day, a scarred old veteran and friend of mine, pulled in right behind me. We got out and walked across the meticulously barbered yard.

"What do you have?" Happy asked the rattled young officer.

"Five bodies," the rookie said. "Three children and two adults. All with gunshot wounds to the head. I've…I've never seen anything like it!"

"What brought this to our attention," Happy asked.

"The woman's boss called when she didn't show up for work this morning. He says they're working on weekends because it's tax season. He asked us to check on her because nobody was answering the phone. And they're *all* dead," Rawlston said again. " *All* of them, Sergeant Wolfe."

"You've seen bodies, before, son," I said, puzzled at the normally calm officer.

"Not like *this*. You have to see it to understand what I mean."

"You didn't touch anything, did you?" Day asked.

"No sir. I didn't."

"You want to come in with me, Wolfe?" the homicide detective asked.

"Sure," I said.

It was the first time I had ever been in their home in the twelve years we had lived beside the pretend family. It was like a hotel room, everything in place, impeccably free of dust—a sterile showplace, just like the yard.

The master bedroom was the first one we came to. Mrs. Pate was on her back, eyes closed, with her arms to her side, as if she had been posed neatly. There was a small bullet hole that looked like a .22 caliber wound in her temple and a plastic garbage bag spread out under her head. She hadn't bled much, indicating a quick death.

The three children were also in their beds, the boys in one room and the girl in another, methodically and neatly laid out, each with a single wound to the temple and with plastic garbage bags in place under their heads. There was very little blood in evidence, though it appeared that blood had been wiped off the oldest boy's headboard, where it had probably spurted before he died.

Captain Pate's body was in the garage. A .22 caliber semi-automatic target pistol was on the work bench, unloaded, freshly cleaned with the magazine laying neatly beside it.

He had put down a plastic tarp in the middle of the garage to protect the floor, and had used a single barrel twelve gauge shotgun to kill himself. I had no doubt that he had calculated and decided that a .22 round might not do the trick quickly enough for a fully conscious man. So he had made certain he would not survive

The barrel of the shotgun had been positioned under his chin and his brain had exploded from the top of his head like a grotesque flower. There were spatters of blood, brain tissue and bone fragments on the unfinished ceiling but not a drop of blood on the floor or walls. I guess he had underestimated slightly, just how far upward the blast would send debris. The most precise of us sometimes miscalculate minor details.

"Jesus," the homicide detective said. "Talk about anally retentive people. You'd think a clean garage floor would have been the last thing he had on his mind when he was getting ready to blow his brains out."

"He was an engineer," I said. "Very meticulous."

In the kitchen, the family financial records were laid out on the table, neatly stacked by category. A quick look at the bank book told us that there was little money in the account, but we never did find any financial problems horrible enough provoke what he had done.

The videotape he had left explained in detail why he had done what he did. When we played it, Captain Pate's round face appeared, business-like and unsmiling, sitting at the kitchen table; the date that appeared on the screen indicated it had been made the day before.

In a nutshell, Captain Pate had decided that his family, because of his inability to find a job in keeping with his educational background— the direct result of an unnamed conspiracy against him, he said—had become the object of ridicule. It was his duty, he said, to protect them at all costs. He had not, it appeared from his words, consulted any of them about their status in the community *or* their feelings about early death.

He explained his plan to make milkshakes (which they seldom enjoyed because Mrs. Pate said sweets were unhealthy) for his entire family, laced with a sedative. After they all became groggy he would send them to their beds and kill them painlessly. He said that he wasn't sure of Heaven, but life on Earth had become Hell. He asked that whoever found them to return the borrowed video camera and pistol to their owners and to see that his brother got the detailed list of final instructions he had left on the kitchen table with his financial records.

When the tape was finished, the homicide detective went into the kitchen and looked in the sink, then opened the dishwasher. "He rinsed off the glasses and the blender and put them in the dishwasher," the detective said. "Want to bet that the empty pill bottle is in the garbage?"

I didn't take the bet.

The Worst Thing I Did in the War

ONCE I KILLED a man, maybe more than one. I'm not sure. It was near a place called Dak To in the old Republic of Vietnam on a hill not important enough to have a real name. The mapmakers just called it Hill 875. The battle started November 19th, 1968 and ended four days later on the 23rd. The man I killed was a North Vietnamese Regular.

I was with A Company, 2nd Battalion, 503rd Airborne Infantry, 173rd Airborne Brigade. The relatively small number of American troops who originally started up the hill thought they were going after a company sized unit, at most—but as it turned out, there were a lot more NVRs than they expected. The ambush our guys walked into was a slaughter. I didn't start up the hill until the second day of fighting.

The last day of the battle, we stormed over the top of the hill with bayonets fixed. We had been so close to the enemy as we inched our way up—sometimes no more than 30 meters apart—I might well have killed men I didn't know about. But the one I shot in the face at point blank range, the one whose head seemed to shrivel like an orange sucked dry before my eyes was the certain kill, and the one I'll never forget.

In modern warfare, soldiers seldom are close enough to see the shock in the eyes of an enemy they have just shot or to hear the gurgling and desperate gasping of dying men as their lungs fill with blood—and finally, to realize just how much blood the human body really contains. It's not something I remember with joy or pride—only terror and relief when it was over and I was still alive.

There were four Medals of Honor awarded for that single battle. Two of them were given posthumously. The 2nd and 4th Battalions of the 503rd Infantry suffered 33 missing in action, 158 killed and 411 evacuated wounded during those three days, while the ground shook like Jell-O as the Air Force pounded the hill, bombs hitting so close that we were as afraid of our own airpower at times as we were of the enemy. I'm told that 3,000 NVRs were killed in that battle, and don't doubt it at all.

Not long ago, I found a picture on the Internet that had been shot from the air over Hill 875, the night after the battle was over. It looked like a scene from hell and brought back memories of the sulfuric smell that hangs over a battlefield. All the trees had been turned into splinters and the smoke was still wafting up in places. It was a new perspective of Hill 875 for me because when I was fighting the battle, all I saw was my little segment of hell and it was a blur, like the memory of a nightmare.

As bad as it was, killing the NVR at close range was not the worst thing I did while I was visiting the now defunct Republic of Vietnam. Not by a long shot. When I look back on my life, the killing makes me sad but it causes no shame. It was what I *had* to. The thing that still festers like an infected wound concerns a little girl who sold popcorn, in as safe a place as there was is in a country that had been a war zone since the mid-1940s, when the North Vietnamese took on the French. What I did to that child will be with me until I die.

I met her only because I was already qualified to be a clerk typist when I arrived in country. I had only scoffed when they offered me a chance to fill an existing vacancy the day I arrived, the day before I went up the hill. I was, by God, a paratrooper! But I didn't let pride keep me from taking that same job as company clerk when it was offered again—two days later when I came down from the hill.

I figured those three days of hell would last me forever and I knew I would be happy to live in relative safety for the rest of my tour, maybe even the rest of my life. During the remainder of my time in country, I typed a lot of paperwork on wounded, dead and missing paratroopers and infantry grunts.

I never knew the little girl's name. When I think of her, it's as the "little popcorn girl at An Khe," which was a small town about half way between Qui Nhon and Pleiku on Highway 19. A lot of units were headquartered there, inside a 12 mile long, 100 yard defensive barrier around the perimeter of the base camp. It's hard to believe but I'm told that today there are few signs that we were ever there.

The reason I don't know her name was because she didn't speak English and I didn't speak Vietnamese. Well, she could say, "*You buy,*

GI?" And I knew the usual smattering of words in her language, or French words that had somehow gotten into her language, such as: *Boocoup,* which means "lots of "or "many," *cam on,* "thank you," *didi,* "get away from me," and *dung lai,* " halt." Most of us were only thinking about going home, not linguistics.

She was Montangard, or more likely, mixed Vietnamese and Montangard blood. The Vietnamese and the tribal mountain people despised each other. To the Vietnamese, the mountain people, many of whom still hunted with spears and arrows during that war, were savages, and to the Montangards, the Vietnamese had always been the invader, trying to drive them from ancestral lands. I'm told that oppression is still going on today.

The little popcorn girl didn't beg, so she was a true Montangard in that respect. Her people had pride.

If a caravan of American troops passed a Montangard warrior on the road and tossed him rations or candy, he would stand as if he hadn't noticed, even if it fell at his feet. I'm told they would pick it up after the troops were out of sight, but I never saw them do it. The little girl never begged, she just sold her popcorn in the paper cones they used in place of bags or cardboard boxes.

There were usually kids following GIs wherever they went, begging for candy and money or offering to pimp their sisters or mothers for a few dollars. That was why I first noticed the little girl. She was ten or eleven and hung back from the other children, her brown eyes alert and filled with a knowledge of things no child should ever have.

She only spoke when I looked at her. "Hey GI, you buy?" The popcorn was 25 cents, if I remember correctly, and I always handed her 50 cents or a dollar because I figured that's how she was feeding herself and maybe her family.

"Hey little lady, you have to be more aggressive if you want to make it in sales," I told her the first time we met. She stared at my face for a moment, trying to read my expression, maybe ready to dodge a kick. When I handed her the dollar bill, took the popcorn and indicated with a wave that I needed no change, she broke into a smile that was like sunshine.

Several times, in the beginning, I tried to give her some of the candy I carried for the other children but she wouldn't take it. The money she would quickly grab and beam a smile up at me. But she came from proud people who didn't take charity. I knew by her eyes she *wanted* the candy badly but would never take it. After a while, I stopped offering.

I still don't understand exactly why I eventually did such a horrible thing to a beautiful little girl who had a smile that lit up the day. I hadn't been raised to do such things. I had been taught to practice the Golden Rule since my own childhood. But eleven months into my twelve month tour, when I was getting short and really worried about being killed, I did it.

It happened because I walked over to where the mail was sorted instead of waiting for it to be delivered. I've always regretted taking that walk.

"Guess you're here to make my job harder, aintcha, hillbilly?" The mail clerk was another Tennessee boy, but he was from Memphis, down on the Mississippi river where the state turns into delta and I was from upper East Tennessee, near the Smoky Mountains National Park in Knoxville, where you are always going up or down because there is no flat country. The boys from Middle and West Tennessee used to make jokes that hillbilly cattle were bred with legs that were shorter on one side than the other so they could comfortably walk around mountains.

Ike Pruitt was the shade of mahogany and wore plastic Army issue glasses with lenses as thick as the bottom of a soft drink bottle. It was like we were from different worlds, the mountains and the delta. We got to be close, though—as close as a black man and a white man could be in a day when the native whores that American soldiers frequented were generally segregated by which race they serviced. Some girls bumped bellies with white soldiers and others with black soldiers but almost never both. The girls didn't really care but many of the soldiers did.

"Just hand me my mail you puny, little wharf rat, and we won't have any problems," I said.

Ike raised his eyebrows above his heavy-lidded, sleepy-looking eyes. "You tryin' to give this little Tennessee nigger trouble, hillbilly? *Real* soldiers like us mail clerks don't take no shit from office warriors like you."

"I just want my mail, flatlander. Hand it over and I'll be on my way."

"Jus' happens I sorted your company's mail already and they's one of them sweet-smellin' letters and envelopes. If they's any good pitchers today, can I see'em?"

"Not in this lifetime, wharf rat." Once, one of the perfumed envelopes had come in with a tear in the side and a very revealing picture of my fiancée had fallen out. I put the new letter under my nose and got a whiff of the honeysuckle perfume that Kellie used to scent her mail. I tore open the thin airmail envelope and unfolded the letter. I was due to arrive back in Knoxville on November the third and our wedding was set for the sixth.

"That girl ain't been writin' as often as she used to, hillbilly," Pruitt said. "You don't think Jody been sniffin' around do ya?" Jody was the guy back home who was *always* after our women. The drill instructors had introduced us to Jody and we had sung about him all through basic training: "*Aint no use in goin' home, Jody's got your girl alone. Sound off, one, two, three, four...*"

I just shook my head and began to read. It only took one paragraph for me to know that I was holding a "Dear John" letter that I had watched my buddies get from the first day of basic training. I had never expected it to happen to me. Kellie and I had been planning our marriage since we were twelve.

"You OK, hillbilly? You just went pale and that's sayin' a lot in your case."

I sat down in a folding chair by the counter, fighting back tears. Kellie's letters had made Vietnam bearable. *How could she have done this to me?* I would have been home in a little more than a month. The next paragraph told me *why*. He was a first year psychology student, just as she was, the letter said. They had just started out studying together, but eventually things had changed. *Fuckin' A, Dick Tracy! Things had changed!* My life had just disintegrated.

"Hillbilly, what's wrong ? Oh man, tell me it's *not* a Dear John. I'm sorry I made that comment about Jody. Just sit a few minutes. Let me get you a beer."

I stood up, knees trembling. I had to get out of the tent before my mask fell off. *A man who had slogged up fuckin' Hill 875 and come down alive couldn't' cry in front of another man—especially not over a woman who had just kissed him off for fuckin' Jody!* I waved the letter in Ike's direction, as casually as I was able, and stepped outside the tent into the sunlight. I stopped and wiped my eyes as if the sun had made them water and started towards my company area, mind whirling like a wind devil. Before I had gone very far, the little popcorn girl appeared as if by magic.

"Hey GI, you buy, *huh?*" She ran along beside me. "You buy?" She extended the paper cone of popcorn in my direction, smiling. "*Good today, GI. Yum. Yum.*" She was smiling, as she had a dozen times before.

Without warning, eleven months of stifled fear and rage erupted and became focused on the little girl's trusting face. I wanted to hurt someone, *anyone.*

It was as if I watched someone else reach out and snatch the popcorn from her hand. Then I ripped the paper cone apart and hurled it at her. Popcorn fell all around her and one piece lodged in her hair. I leaned forward until my face was level with hers.

"Get the fuck away from me you little *gook bitch!*" I couldn't have hurt her more by kicking her. I watched the pain and shock work across her face as she backed up to get out of range. A moment later, she was gone.

Almost without conscious effort, I turned to the right and headed for a place I knew about but had never visited. I had a desire to get drunk on the tiger piss that passed for Vietnamese beer. And I *needed* a woman. It had been a year for me because I had been faithful to the girl back home, probably long after she had spread her legs for somebody else. *What a fool I had been!*

THE NEXT MORNING, I walked down to the area where the little popcorn girl usually worked, despite my throbbing head. Most of the night before was a blur. A couple of MPs had taken me back to my company area in the early morning hours. They knew I was a short-timer because I told them and short-timers had a lot of slack cut for them. Nobody wanted to die so or see anyone else die so close to getting out of country

I wanted to tell the little popcorn girl I was sorry that I had betrayed her, that I had behaved no better than so many others who had hurt her before. More than anything I had ever wanted, I wanted to make thing's *right* with her, so that look of betrayal in her dark eyes would not be the last thing I remembered about her. But I never saw her again.

Maybe she deliberately avoided me; I just don't know. Maybe her family moved on. I spent the rest of my short time in-country watching for her serious little face in the crowds of children following soldiers from place to place. But I knew she wouldn't be in a crowd, begging for attention. She had pride.

The Last Drive-In Movie

DRIVE-IN MOVIES HAVE pretty much gone the way of the dinosaur here in East Tennessee. The last one in Knoxville went out of business around 1984, when I was still a rookie cop. I don't know what finally did them in, whether it was VCRs, the rising price of property or a combination of the two. I miss them.

When baby boomers first started driving there was still a sort of neo-Puritanism that had come along after World War II, and hung around waiting for Woodstock to turn the country upside-down. We didn't have sex education in the 1960s, at least not south of the Mason-Dixon.

Most of our parents couldn't look us in the face and talk about sex and they sure as hell didn't want teachers giving us ideas—as if any kid ever needed anyone to inspire curiosity—so mostly my generation learned the general theory from older kids. The drive-in theater was where most of us got our *real* introduction to the birds and the bees.

I once read somewhere that a majority of young women who came of age in the fifties and sixties lost their virginity straddling their partners in the front seat of a car, not in the old missionary position. Maybe that's why the kids of my generation loved the drive-in movies and were willing to overlook the steamed up car windows in the winter and the scorching heat in the summers before most cars had air-conditioning—not to mention the exorbitant prices we paid for soft drinks and popcorn even by the standards of that day.

It was because I was a rookie cop that I was picked for a stakeout at the last drive-in theater in Knox County, which by that time had deteriorated from its glory days into a place that showed triple-X-rated films. The vice unit needed a couple of fresh faces, a man and a woman, so that's how I ended up partnering with Dorothy Jane

Brown, DJ for short, who despised me. Her animosity had started at the state police academy outside of Nashville while we were both basic recruits.

DJ was beautiful in a country-western sort of way. Even when she really dolled herself up, the outfit usually included cowboy boots and a vest. She was a petite woman with red hair that moved in a rippling fashion and fell almost to her waist when she didn't have it pinned up so her uniform hat would cover it.

She was a natural athlete who ran the mile faster than most male officers, even the very young ones. I wasn't one of the very young ones, having entered law enforcement when I was almost thirty-five years old. It didn't make her any more tolerable that she could also outshoot and out drive almost every male officer at the academy. Maybe it was a trace of jealousy or resentment that caused me to embarrass her. I'm not sure.

We were lined up for our first class in hand to hand combat when the event happened. DJ had been paired with another female officer of comparable size and immediately took exception.

"I'm not going to be arresting a lot of women on the streets," she said. "I want a male partner to make things more realistic." Things grew quiet in the gymnasium.

"Officer Brown," the instructor said, "few arrests are made by brute force. Most suspects will submit to arrest and if it appears they don't intend to, you will call for back-up. The biggest man in this class can't handcuff the smallest without a little cooperation and a few tricks I am going to teach you." The instructor had taught hand to hand combat to special forces troops before retiring from the military. He was a tall, husky man with graying temples.

"I don't care. It's *obvious* that you purposely paired me with another woman. I'd like to change partners," she said.

"Officer Brown, if you'll look around, you'll see that I have also paired the men off according to size because it makes things easier when you first start," the instructor replied.

"I don't care..." she began, just before I butted in without an invitation.

"What he is too much of a gentleman to say, DJ, is that the oldest sickest man in this class would kick your ass in a *real* fight, because size and upper body strength really *do* make a difference."

A titter ran through the assembled class and the instructor fought back a smile. DJ's face turned blood red and it was the only time I ever saw her at a loss for words. She glared at me, bit down on her lower lip and took a position in front of her female partner. It was obvious she didn't trust herself to speak. In fact, she stopped speaking to me altogether—right up to the moment she found out we were to be partners at very close quarters.

"Let me get this straight," DJ said to the vice squad supervisor, right after she found out what our assignment was. "You want me to snuggle up in the front seat of a car with this *Neanderthal*. Is that correct?" We had both been told to show up in casual clothes, the kind a couple might wear on date, but nothing else.

"That's right, Officer Brown. It was the luck of the draw—or in your case, maybe it's just your day in the barrel." The vice sergeant looked like a homeless person. His shirt was ragged, his jeans threadbare, gray hair long and unkempt and his shoes run down at the heels. I had heard he was very good at what he did. "Your captains gave me the names. I just asked for two fresh faces. If you don't think you can do it..."

"I didn't say *that*. I'd rather cuddle up with a poisonous viper but I can do anything you assign me."

"How 'bout you, Blake—got any objections to cuddling with Officer Brown tonight." He raised one bushy eyebrow in an ironic fashion.

"None at all, Sergeant. I have no problem with Officer Brown. The animosity is strictly one way."

"Well, I'm glad both of you can be *professional*. What we have is a perp working the Chapman Highway Drive-in—a man we think—sneaking around the cars, reaching through windows and stabbing women in the butt with a sharp object."

"I've never arrested a piquerist." I said.

"A *what?*" DJ asked.

"A piquerist, DJ. A guy who gets off penetrating the flesh of women—with knives, bullets, teeth and other sharp instruments. It was right there among the definitions of sexual deviants when we went through the academy." I said.

"I suppose I wasn't as interested in sexual deviants when I was at the academy as you were, Officer Blake," she shot back.

"*Moving right along*," the sergeant continued, "we want the two of

you to stake out the theater and see if you can catch the pervert. Think
you can stop squabbling long enough to do it?"

We both nodded affirmatively and the sergeant said, "Good. Set
your radios to J, you'll be all alone on that channel so there won't be
any radio chatter to alert whoever is doing this. Go by the service
center and pick up the gold, compact Chrysler. Here are the keys.
Good luck."

I WAS ALREADY filling the tank of the old compact Chrysler when she
pulled her cruiser into the service center. As she locked her car up and
walked across the lot, I furtively watched her from the corner of my
eye. She was wearing tight blue jeans, sandals and a yellow tee shirt
that said: "BEYOND BITCH." She carried a small purse over her
shoulder on a long strap. DJ Brown filled out a pair of jeans nicely.
She stood, arms crossed and watched me put the cap back on the gas
tank.

"Have you had dinner yet?" I asked.

"No, I haven't."

"Would you like to stop somewhere and eat?" I asked. She stared
at me, as if having a hard time assimilating what I had said.

"We've got plenty of time. If you have no objection, I'd like to stop
at Wong's on Chapman Highway and eat. They have the best hot and
sour soup I've ever eaten."

"I have no objections." She went around and got into the passenger
side. A moment later, I sat down under the steering wheel and started
the engine.

"Would you prefer to drive? I asked.

"No. *Everyone* knows the man drives in this part of the country.
It's the way society works here in the South. If I drove, it might blow
our cover."

We chugged out to the street, black smoke boiling out of the
exhaust pipe. The old car sounded like a tractor—just the kind of car
that would blend right in at the last drive-in theater in Knox County,
a place that showed only triple X films.

"Hopefully, we won't need any speed tonight," I said. "I used this
car on a drug buy and it won't pull the hat off your head." It was
obvious I was making an effort to be civil, but she wasn't making it any
easier.

"That's good, though. Nobody will notice us unless a cop stops us for the loud muffler," I said with a chuckle.

"How do you like working the DUI car?" she asked, not bothering to acknowledge my attempt at humor.

"Well, I like the night shift and there's never a shortage of drunk drivers. I stay busier than I like sometimes."

"Some of the old-timers on my shift are calling you a squirrel because you make so many arrests. Is that true? *Are* you a squirrel, Blake?" She seemed to be gouging at me, trying to get a rise. In police jargon, at least in Knox County at that time, a "squirrel" was somebody who took a lot of risks, made too many traffic stops and even worked over when he didn't have to.

"I've got eight hours to fill on every shift and since I don't answer calls for service, it makes the time pass. The arrests add up, I guess."

"Is there really such a thing as a piquerist, or were you pulling my leg?"

"It *really* was on the list of perversions they gave us at the academy, but I tried to research it once and I found that most shrinks say it doesn't really exist. I only found one case where piquerism was used to actually convict anybody. It was a case that happened back in 1981, where this high school senior named Robie Drake up in New York murdered two of his classmates on a lover's lane."

"Did you used to be a college professor, Blake? Some of the guys on my shift say you sound like a college professor when you testify." I tried to take a read and see if she was being deliberately hostile or just herself. Her long black hair, worn down that night framed her dark blue, almost purple eyes. She looked very young at that moment.

"No, I just do my homework before I go to court. I've done a lot of other things, but I'm not a professor. In fact, I've never been to college."

"Can I ask you something else?"

"Sure." I shrugged. "I may not answer it, but you're free to ask."

"Do you hate women in general or just me in particular?"

"Neither. I like women as much or more than the average heterosexual male."

I took the I-75 exit onto the downtown loop to get on Henley Street, which turned into Chapman Highway on the other side of the Henley Street bridge. Isolated somewhat by the Tennessee River,

South Knoxville had a distinct personality. Sometimes we would jokingly ask for a Green Card when we arrested people from South Knoxville in other parts of Knox County.

"You really embarrassed me at the academy that day." Her cheeks flushed a bit at the memory.

"I'm sorry about that. I shouldn't have said it—but you were a little hard to take sometimes with your rah, rah siz ba boom attitude. No offense. And maybe I felt a little threatened because you were so good at everything."

"It's hard being a woman in a man's world."

"I'm sure it is, DJ."

"We have to be twice as good to be accepted, you know."

"Maybe it won't always be that way. Times are changing and women like you are changing them."

I glanced at her and saw that she was blushing. "It's very nice of you to say that," she replied." But we're *still* not even."

"I understand completely. Pay back is a bitch. No pun intended."

"I guess we got off to a bad start Blake." She shook her head and smiled. "But I *still* owe you one."

"Gotcha, DJ. Dinner's on me, then. A peace offering."

WE LEFT WONG'S, well fed and satisfied. I had not exaggerated. At the time, Wong's served the best hot and sour soup I had ever eaten. Later, his wife divorced him and married his top chef. She later opened another restaurant in North Knoxville which thereafter had the best hot and sour soup I had ever eaten.

"The food was very good, Officer Blake. Thanks for dinner. It's the first time I ever tried Chinese food in a restaurant. I didn't know if I'd like it or not." DJ said.

"How did you manage to live twenty-five years or so without trying Chinese cuisine?"

"I'm only twenty-four. Have you ever heard of Egypt, Kentucky, Blake?"

"No. I can't say that I have."

"It's a wide place in the road. My grandmother raised me there. She had no car, she was a religious fanatic in the Pentecostal Holiness Church and she didn't let me date at all. I was never really on my own before I started my junior year at the University of Tennessee. As a matter of fact, I'm still catching up on what most people take for granted—like television."

"You grew up without television? That's child abuse."

"You don't know the half of it. I didn't see a movie, except in school, until I was nineteen. Tonight will be the first pornographic film I've *ever* seen. I've led a sheltered life."

"Why didn't you tell the sergeant? I'm sure he would have understood."

"Sure, he would've understood—and then told everyone else about it so they could understand, too. I always meant to get around to seeing a dirty movie, but there were a lot of things ahead of pornography on my list, Blake."

"I see your point. It's just hard to believe…"

"Yes, it is. That's why I expect you to keep it confidential," DJ said.

"What happens in this cruiser stays in this cruiser, DJ."

"That hasn't been my experience," she said. "I found out early that men like to boast about… conquests."

"Not all men, DJ." She looked at me from the corner of her eye with a slight lift of the eyebrow. I decided to change the subject.

"So, why did you become a cop?"

"Well, there was a scholarship in criminal justice available at the little community college I attended. By my junior year, I really was interested in criminology." She shrugged. "I had intended to eventually start graduate school but money was short so I became a cop. I got here just as the powers-that-be decided they needed more female officers. That was three years ago. Now I'm a cop through and through."

"Here we are," I said, turning across the highway towards the shabby, old drive-in theater, where the back of the screen stood like a mountain, covered with kudzu. "Just in time, the sun is going down." I pulled up to the booth and a bored woman in her fifties put down her cigarette long enough to take my money and hand me two tickets.

"I guess you remember this place before it started showing triple-X films," DJ said.

"I was here a few times but I was a North Knoxville boy. I went to the Skyway, Sunset and Family Drive-ins."

"There were that many drive-in theaters around here?" she asked.

"You should pull over to the left. We stand a better chance of the pervert approaching us over there where it's dark."

I followed her instructions. "I think there were six or eight drive-in theaters in this county at one time. Drive-in movies were recreation and sex education rolled into one for my generation."

"You make it sound as if you're ancient. How old are you?" she asked.

"Thirty-eight in a couple of weeks."

"You've got 14 years on me. That's not a lot of difference," she said.

"Maybe it just seems like a long time. I've been married for sixteen years and the Vietnam War took a chunk out of my life." I reached out and got the speaker from the metal pole by the car and the sound came on as if on cue.

"Talk about good timing," DJ said. "Put your arm up so I can pretend to cuddle."

"Roll down your window first," I said. "It will be sweltering in here with the air conditioner off."

She rolled the window down, then slid over close to me. The odor of lavender floated up to my nostrils, and I smelled her shampoo. It was the same as my wife used. I put my arm up on the back of the seat. I felt an unfamiliar stirring in my stomach. I had been nineteen the last time a young woman who was not my wife had gotten so close. I reminded myself that I was on the job and DJ was just another cop. But my hormones remained unconvinced.

"Don't get any ideas, Blake."

"I... DJ, I wouldn't do *that*." I thought she had read my mind.

"Lighten up. Officer Blake. I was joking."

"I *knew* that."

"Geez, they don't waste time on preliminaries, do they?" My partner said. The giant screen was suddenly filled with a woman's lips enthusiastically administering oral sex to a man with a freakishly large penis. I heard DJ take a deep breath.

"It's pretty gross the first time you see an explicit porno film," I said, feeling a little embarrassed for her. It had to be difficult for a country girl.

"I'm a *professional*, Blake. Don't worry about me. Just keep your eyes peeled for the creeper. Don't want him to slip up on anybody— especially me."

DJ's eyes, I noticed, were fixed on the screen where the couple had changed roles and the man had his face buried in the crotch of a bleached blonde woman who was groaning in an excellent monotone.

In the course of ten minutes, the couple ran through the gamut of, doggy style, woman on top and anal sex. The first couple was joined by an Asian woman who knelt down beside them and took one of the blonde's nipples in her mouth.

Almost simultaneously, I felt DJ's right hand close on my groin. It was my turn to gasp. "DJ..." Her left hand grabbed the back of my neck and her mouth covered mine before I could get out another word. I felt her tongue probing between my lips. I managed to pull back long enough to speak, as she lifted her tee shirt.

"DJ... we shouldn't be doing this." I didn't sound convincing.

"We *have* to put on a good show, Blake. Act like a *professional!*" Once more her soft, hot mouth covered mine and this time her tongue pushed it's way in without resistance. I pulled her closer and pushed her bra out of my way. Her nipples felt like ripe blackberries under my palm.

"*Oh yes, Blake* ...put on a *good* show!"

I needed no more encouragement. I had known that some women were driven into a frenzy by visual pornography, just like some of their male counterparts. I had even known a couple. But never in my most hormonally charged fantasies had I ever suspected that DJ would be one of them. It was apparent that she had never suspected it either.

"Yes *baby*, let's make this look *good*—like real professionals!" Without warning she was tugging at the zipper of my jeans.

"DJ, we're taking this too far," I said, even as I slid down further into the seat so she could get my jeans open. She ignored what I had said and I felt her fingers reach inside my clothes and free me from the confines of the jeans and jockey shorts.

"Oh yeah, baby, look at you all hard and standing straight up for DJ. Hold your breath. I'm going to make this look *really* professional!"

"Yes, sweetheart, make it look good!" I leaned back in the seat and waited for nirvana. The pain of anticipation was exquisite. At that moment, however, an arm snaked through the lowered passenger side window and stabbed DJ in her beautiful, heart-shaped ass with something sharp.

My eyes opened as I heard her sharp intake of breath. Then, as

DJ's high-pitched screech of pain and indignation pierced my right ear, I saw a dark figure dart around the front of the car. I clawed at the door handle with one hand, trying to zip my jeans at the same time.

"Get that *sonofabitch!*" DJ yelled, pulling her bra and blouse down. As I got the car door opened, I heard DJ calling for back-up on the portable.

Our piquerist might well have gotten away but he got his foot caught in kudzu vines growing by the tumble-down fence as he ran like a gazelle towards the back exit. He hit the ground hard, but was back on his feet in an instant. I was under an adrenaline rush and closed the distance between us after he fell.

He tried to leap across the small creek running under the bridge at the back side of the theater, but I caught him by his long hair and jerked him to a halt. Without warning, he swung his right arm towards me and I felt something pierce my left shoulder all the way to the bone. I would later learn that it was indeed an old-fashioned hat pin.

"You perverted *bastard!*" I yelled, smashing the palm of my hand into his face, causing a spray of blood from his flattened nose. A moment later I was sitting on his chest, slapping his face back and forth like a ping pong ball when DJ grabbed my arm.

"Stop it, Blake. You're going to *kill* him!"

I stopped slapping him and by the time I caught my breath, a patrol unit was on the scene and the prisoner was being cuffed.

I WAS SITTING on a gurney at Baptist Hospital, my arm stinging from a tetanus shot, a small bandage covering the place on my shoulder where the hat pin had penetrated, when DJ came into the small trauma room. Down the hall, I could hear our prisoner whining and complaining about police brutality as the doctor stuffed his nose with waxed string to reshape it where I had flattened it earlier. He probably thought I had been enraged because he had stuck me. DJ and I both knew better.

"You all right?" she asked, eyes downcast.

"Yeah, I'll live. How about you?"

"My ass is sore and I'm embarrassed beyond belief by what happened in the car. Other than that, I'm fine," she said.

"*Nothing* happened in the car that was out of the ordinary, DJ."

I didn't look her directly in the eye. "If the dirt bag says anything different, nobody will believe him. Especially if they know the kind of relationship we had before tonight."

"I know you aren't going to *tell* anyone, but I'm still embarrassed. It was very unprofessional."

"DJ, if what happened tonight is the most unprofessional thing you ever do, you'll never have a reason to be ashamed."

"You're a decent man, Blake. I'm sorry I misjudged you." She was still not looking me directly in the eye.

"What happened in the car, stays in the car. Don't worry about it," I told her.

She started to say something else but didn't. She turned and walked out and we never mentioned the incident again.

I have to admit, though, that even today, if I see DJ and she's wearing something that's form-fitting, I get a little aroused. If I allow myself to dwell on it for more than a few seconds, I get *really* aroused.

She's a beautiful woman in a country-western sort of way.

Gypsy Queen With the Big Red Heart

CHARLES TINDELL TWISTED irritably in the leather bucket-seat of his Mercedes, angry at the traffic that had delayed him thirty minutes. He had no real reason for hurrying home, but was irritated and flushed just the same.

Sally would be on her third Tequila Sunrise, slack-mouthed and slurred of speech, when he arrived. Or worse, she would be dressed and ready to go out, all lacquered nails, capped teeth and enamel glitter.

The glitter had at first appeared to be a natural sparkle, twenty years ago, but the facade had not lasted very long into the marriage. It was poetic justice, he supposed. Sally's main attraction had not been her looks or personality, but a father on the board of directors of the bank where Charles Tindell had worked as an ambitious, young teller.

The banker's eyes fell on the bumper of the ten-year-old Ford ahead of him. On one side was a sticker that said: ABORTION KILLS. On the opposite side was one that said: ELVIS LIVES. Charles wondered if the two bumper stickers were supposed to have a mutual significance. The driver of the old car was lost in conversation with someone on his cell phone.

Charles speculated as to whether the man in the beat-up old Ford dreaded going home to *his* wife. If so, the banker decided, a divorce would be easy enough for a man who owned nothing to speak of—unlike Tindell who stood to lose a fortune if he left home and hearth.

He fished around in the pocket of his cashmere jacket for his cigarettes and the special holder which was supposed to cut down his nicotine a little at a time until he could quit. All it had done, so far, was cause him to smoke more in an effort to get the same amount of nicotine.

The problem was that he had no *real* desire to stop smoking, even though his doctor said that high blood pressure and clogged arteries were going to kill him. Smoking was his only vice, and Charles Tindell, solid citizen, Presbyterian elder, Sunday school teacher and senior president of the Northside Citizens Bank thought every man deserved at least one bad habit.

The cigarettes were not in the pockets of the cashmere jacket or in either of his shirt pockets. With another surge of anger, he remembered that he had left them on his desk at work.

To the right he saw a flashing sign that proclaimed, in neon splendor, EARL'S MARKET. Smaller, painted letters declared that the market sold: *Sandwiches, Beer, Cigarettes, Hotdogs, Magazines* and *Groceries.*

Charles had never been in the little market, though he knew it was part of a chain that did business with one of his branch offices. He pulled in and found a parking place among the battered old cars and shiny new ones. Earl's Market evidently had some kind of attraction that cut across socioeconomic lines.

Inside, he smelled sliced ham and corned beef from the deli section and was reminded of the small general stores of his childhood, where you could buy meat and cheese by the slice. There were also a few dusty shelves of canned goods, but to the trained eye of a banker it was evident that the market's main sources of revenue came from the fully stocked beer coolers and the pinball machines in the back.

There were ten such machines with garish, cartoon-like pictures on tall, glass, where lights and numbers flashed in kaleidoscopic colors. The pinball machines were all in use by tense men, hunched up close, leaning forward like pieces in a matched set, rhythmically squeezing the flipper buttons on the sides, as silver balls slithered, banged and clanged against lighted domes and bars.

There were no trendy video games at Earl's Market, no warriors battling on computer screens or cars racing through cyber space. The pinball machines were of the old-fashioned variety from Tindell's youth, the genuine article, ordered from a place that specialized in all kinds of antiques. Earl was a closet nostalgia buff.

Nobody else in Knox County had them, except in private game rooms. They were expensive but responsible for most of Earl's cash flow. The varied themes pictured on the glass behind the pinball machines—such as *The Indy 500, Fort Apache, The Twilite Zone, The*

Roaring Twenties—were all different, but the purpose of each machine was the same.

Charles would have known that purpose, even if he had not noticed the wide range of clothing—from business suits to dirty poplin—that corresponded to the disparity in price among the cars parked outside. The pinball machines were obviously gambling devices, thinly veiled as recreational machines.

During his two-year stint in the army, Charles had become well acquainted with the obsessive, fevered glint in the eyes of gamblers. He had learned that the type of game does not matter to an addict—only the risk.

"A pack of Winstons," he told the short, bald clerk, still watching the pinball players, grinding and twisting against the machines. Stale cigarette smoke had formed a carpet in the air above them. Evidently, neither Earl nor his customers worried about secondhand smoke. Charles took his cigarettes and change from the clerk and started to leave. The machine at the very back of the room caught his attention, however.

It was the picture on the glass screen that drew his gaze. Across the top were flashing letters proclaiming *Gypsy Queen.* The eyes in the face of the woman painted on the glass seemed to be looking directly at Charles Tindell. It was a face from his dreams, a girl once glimpsed from a bus window in Greenwich Village when he was a young soldier on leave—a face never forgotten, a face often remembered in his fantasies on the rare occasions when he still made a dispassionate, rigid form of love to his wife.

The Gypsy Queen's Slavic features were almost, but not quite, Asian, as if there was some lingering trace of a Mongol warrior who had once cohabited with a fair European woman in the dim mists of time. Black hair cascaded to her waist. There was a frank, earthy look about her—the exact opposite of his own blonde, aging ice maiden, waiting with a drink in her hand for him to come home to a scented and over-decorated house he had come to despise.

A gangling boy of eighteen or so, slapped the side of the machine in disgust as brazen-sounding bells went off and letters appeared under the Gypsy Queen's right breast, declaring *tilt.* The boy walked away angrily, cursing under his breath.

The clerk watched curiously as the trim, well-manicured man with stylish gray at the temples walked over to the Gypsy Queen and hesitantly dropped in a quarter left from the cigarette change. The man stepped back, startled as the lights, whistles and bells came to life. He cautiously sent a silver ball skittering down the runway. It careened like a quicksilver streak from side to side, then went directly to the hole closest to the front and dropped in.

"Beginners luck," the clerk said to himself as numbers flashed, raising the odds on the machine. By the time the fourth ball in a row had dropped into place, not only the clerk, but also several spectators had gathered around the machine as jangling bells announced that the *Gypsy Queen* was giving up a jackpot.

The pinball addicts buzzed among themselves, but the well-heeled businessman seemed unimpressed. In fact, his eyes had not left the Gypsy Queen's face. A bright red heart behind her rounded left breast began to flash off and on, becoming visible behind the white peasant's blouse, as the fifth ball lined up, turning the jangling of bells and the flashing of colored lights into a cacophony of light and sound.

"Don't," one of the addicts, a round, little man in a ball cap said, just as the banker was about to drop in another quarter. "Go get your payoff before you put in another coin. That big red flashing heart means that you hit the *super* jackpot."

"Payoff?"

"Yeah. You just won a hundred bucks. I've never seen anybody hit *that* machine for five straight balls. Go up to the counter and Slick will give you the money."

"Excuse me," Charles said, a moment later, to the bald, little man behind the counter who had been identified as Slick, "but someone told me that I just won a hundred dollars."

"*Strictly* speakin', since gamblin' *is* illegal except in certain places—and this not bein' one of them—you just won four hundred free games." He handed Charles five crisp twenty dollar bills and winked at him.

"Could I have this in quarters please?" Charles asked, totally shocked at his own behavior. It wouldn't do for a man of his stature in the community to be seen playing pinball in a seedy, little all-night market.

He was exhilarated, though. The skinny youth had pounded on the Gypsy and she had scorned him. Charles had treated her with gentle respect and she had responded by rewarding him.

Three hours later, Charles had put the entire hundred dollars back in the machine. He glanced at his watch, stunned at the lapse of time. Regretfully, he took one last look at the Gypsy Queen and left the market. He was whistling as he drove home that evening. It had been fun, a rare commodity in his life. Of course, it was a one-time thing.

He was still telling himself that the next day—almost until the moment he pulled on to the lot of Earl's Market, just after work.

"How much is he into us for, Slick?" Earl asked.

A hulking brute of a man with a face flattened by long ago prize fights, Earl was a merchant with a total and unconditional belief in the corruption of all men. He sold beer and gambling in a relaxed atmosphere and did not begrudge his customers the twenty percent that his machines were set to give back. The twenty percent kept them playing. Those who tried to cheat Earl by tampering with his machines, however, lived to regret it.

"Nothin' really. He's already put the whole hundred bucks back in. When he hit the jackpot two nights in a row, I decided I'd better call. I checked the Gypsy after he left last night. He hadn't drilled into it and I didn't see any way he coulda been usin' magnets. It's like the machines *payin'* him to play."

"Slick, do you believe in magic?" Earl asked, rolling the cigar in his mouth.

"No, why?"

"Because, If it ain't magic, he's found a way to screw us. That machine *can't* pay more than twenty percent. If he ain't cheatin' us, magic's the only other explanation. That machine's a mechanical device. It ain't got a mind of it's own."

"What should I do?" Slick asked.

"Nothin', not until I get the tag number on that Mercedes and find out who he is. Don't take a rocket scientist to see money written all over him, does it? We got to be discreet. Let him play tonight, no matter how much he wins. After he leaves, get Catfish in here and have him take that machine apart and find out what's wrong?."

"Gotcha covered, Boss," Slick replied.

THE FOLLOWING MORNING, Charles Tindell did not go to work; he went straight to Earl's Market and waited impatiently while another customer lost ten dollars to the Gypsy, then, with a smile of satisfaction, dropped in his quarter and looked up at her face.

Since beginning his brief relationship with the Gypsy Queen, he had not spent more than twenty-five cents of his own money. After the first quarter, the Gypsy Queen kept paying him to play—periodically flashing the big, red heart behind her full breast to declare him a *super* winner. As usual, after the first five balls, the heart was flashing.

When Slick went into work on the second shift, eight hours later, and found Charles Tindell there ahead of him, he decided that he'd better call Earl. The banker was not acting right. He was crooning to the machine like a lunatic, caressing the sides, his face red as a pickled beet. Something was definitely wrong with the obviously wealthy man and Slick didn't want Earl to blame him if something bad happened.

The well-dressed man seemed to deteriorate before Slick's eyes as the afternoon wore on. Cigarette ashes had begun to pile up on his cashmere jacket and his fly was still open from the last hurried trip to the restroom. His tie was loose and his formerly fashionably styled gray hair was mussed and hanging over his eyes. By the time Earl arrived, the banker had won and lost three hundred more dollars.

"Well?" Slick asked as his boss came in and leaned against the counter. "Who is he?"

"*That*," Earl said, chewing his cigar, "is the man who holds the mortgage on all my markets."

"No shit?" Slick sounded impressed.

"Yeah," Earl replied. "How much is he into us for?"

"Still even," Slick answered with a shrug. "Catfish said there wasn't nothin' wrong with the machine last night, but he changed the odds on it, anyway. It should only be payin' off *ten* percent today, but I can't see nothin' different. He keeps winnin' and losin' a hundred bucks at a time.

As they watched, Charles Tindell reluctantly left the machine and hurried to the rest-room. As soon as he was out of sight, a pimply youth with tight blue jeans stepped up and dropped in a quarter. Two minutes later, the banker stood behind him, fists clenched in rage.

"Get away from the Gypsy Queen!" Charles Tindell hissed menacingly.

The boy turned and sneered. "*You* get away from here, old man. This ain't your machine. I already dropped in my quarter."

Without warning, Charles Tindell grabbed the boy by his greasy hair and slung him to the floor. As the boy landed on his back, the banker pitched a quarter at him. There was a look of total shock in the boy's, as if he couldn't believe what had happened.

"There's your money back. Don't touch the Gypsy again."

Without speaking, the pimply youth got up and left hurriedly. He didn't understand what was happening and didn't want to stay long enough to find out. The old dude was strong, really strong.

"He's crazy," Slick said quietly.

"Yeah, it looks like I'm gonna *have* to do somethin'," Earl said with a sigh, dropping his cigar on the floor and grinding it with his foot, "whether I want to or not. Maybe I'll sell it to him. Hell, I'll *give* it to him, if he'll just go home."

He started towards the banker, then stopped, fascinated, as the man sent the silver balls skittering in rapid succession, seemingly paying no attention to what he was doing, eyes fixed on the picture of the *Gypsy Queen*. The metal balls all dropped into the proper holes as if guided by a hidden radar. The bells and lights, including the big red heart began to flash and jangle.

"That's all right, baby," Charles Tindell whispered. "I won't let him put his filthy hands on you again. Do it for me, Gypsy. Make me happy. *Do it for me!*"

Earl stood, mouth open, as the banker ground his pelvis against the pinball machine, seemingly in ecstasy. Then, without warning, the banker stiffened, jerked spasmodically in a parody of orgasmic dance and collapsed on the floor, a dribble of saliva coming from the corner of his mouth.

"Oh shit," Earl said. "Call an ambulance, Slick!"

"WHAT DID THEY say at the emergency room?" Slick asked, as he and Earl watched Catfish tinker in the electronic guts of the Gypsy Queen.

"His heart went out," Earl replied. "His old lady was more pissed about him dyin' in a dump like this, than she was about him dyin'. Real icy bitch. I could almost understand why he preferred bein' here with the Gypsy Queen."

"Goes to show, I guess," Slick said.

"What?"

"Bein' rich don't make you happy."

"Yeah," Earl replied. "But I always wanted to find out."

"I saw you pattin' him down for tools before the ambulance got here. Did you find a drill or magnets?" Slick asked.

"Nope, not a thing," Earl replied, a distant look on his face.

"Hey, Earl," Catfish yelled from across the room, "come over here."

"What is it?" the big man asked, lumbering across the room, followed by the faithful Slick. The disheveled technician was staring, as if perplexed, at a black lump behind the glass panel of the Gypsy Queen.

"This machine was in *perfect* condition yesterday. I checked *all* the circuits. *Somethin'* sure as hell went wrong today, though. *Look.*" Leaning forward, the two of them saw that the wire supplying current to the bulb in the heart-shaped holder had melted and that the heat had cracked the red plastic cover in half."

"Be damned," Earl said, "a broken heart."

"Well, no matter. I can fix it." Catfish told him.

"Naw, just get rid of it," Earl said, lighting the stub of a cigar between his teeth. "I don't think it'll ever work right for anyone else again, no matter what you do to it."

"I don't understand," Catfish said with a puzzled expression.

"Do you believe in magic?" Earl asked the technician. Without waiting for an answer, the store owner bit down on the cigar he had been chewing on, then turned and left

And Life Stands Explained

"So, THE WORLD stands on your shoulders today? You should change your name to Atlas, maybe. Now *he* had reason for a backache—but a young man like you, it couldn't hurt to be out laughing with the girls and enjoying life," the booming voice said in lightly accented words that sounded—at least to my untrained Appalachian ears—European, probably German.

I looked up, somewhat irritated at having been distracted from my self-pity—and in the reading section at the main branch of Knoxville's Lawson-McGhee Library. A library should be a place of refuge.

The speaker was a stocky, a little past middle age, with a sort of Spencer Tracy air; the Spencer Tracy of later years, of course, not the young leading man. He was wearing a black wool overcoat and a black felt hat that brought the word "fedora" to mind, even though I knew nothing about hats. My expression must have shown my annoyance because he immediately apologized.

"Sorry, young man. I didn't mean to come on like a *nudnik*," he said, his voice a little less loud than before, but not much.

"A what?" I asked.

"A *nudnik*," he replied. It's Yiddish for an old nag, especially a monumentally boring one."

"That's all right. I didn't mean to be rude either. You're right, though. I do feel like the world is standing on my shoulders right now."

He sat down and unwound a checkered wool scarf from around his neck, took off the black hat and leather gloves and laid them on the table. I looked for a cane with a gold head, but none was forthcoming.

"My name is Jacob Goldstein," he said, extending his right hand. "I'm a rabbi by trade, which makes me a professional *nudnik* sometimes"

I smiled at that and shook his hand firmly. "Then my father is also a professional *nudnik*. He's the pastor of a Baptist Church, and so are my two older brothers, three uncles and four cousins—not to mention my grandfather and *his* father. By the way, my name is John Stamey."

"So, John Stamey, every time your family has a gathering there is a *minyon* of professional religionists," my new acquaintance said, shaking his head. For the first time I noticed that his neatly combed hair was completely white and that his eyes were a smoky, indistinct color, like fog over a mountain.

"I'm sorry, a *what?*"

"A *minyon*," he said, "is the ten Jews required for a religious service. There is an old saying among my people that nine saints can't make a *minyon*—unless a cobbler joins them. My people tend to view rabbis with less awe than Christians do their priests and ministers."

"I don't know about that," I replied. "My father says that a Baptist pastor's authority lies somewhere between the deacon board and the church janitor."

"Your father sounds like a man who knows how to laugh at himself, a *mentsh*." Seeing the curiosity in my eyes he immediately explained himself. "A *mentsh* is a fine fellow, someone to emulate. I'll try to stop with the Yiddish. I forget that not everyone grew up listening to it."

"That's all right, I find it interesting. And you're right. My father's a good man—but he has his blind spots."

"Don't we all?" he asked.

"I suppose so."

"So, John, is your problem with your father then?" His right eyebrow went up quizzically.

"Yeah, sort of. It's bigger than that, though. It's about my *whole* life."

Without warning, I felt a soothing sensation within my chest. It was as if a boil had just been lanced and relief was flooding through me. I realized that the relief was nothing more than the result of opening my mouth to ventilate. I had not actually said anything important, but I knew I was going to.

"Mr. Goldstein, could I buy your lunch?" Immediately, I wondered if I had committed a faux pas. "It's a few blocks, but we can go down to Harold's Deli on Gay Street. I mean, if…"

"You want to know if I eat kosher? The answer is yes and no. Like with most Reform Jews today, I don't eat pork, but I've been known to dig into a lobster tail—even though it has no fins or scales.

"You know what kosher means, John?"

"Not really." I said.

"In the *strict* sense, it means food prepared exactly by Jewish dietary laws. More loosely, it means food has been *properly* prepared or is fit to eat. And I can tell you, lobster tail properly prepared is *definitely* fit to eat." He roared with laughter at his own humor, causing studious heads to turn in irritation.

"Well, I can't afford lobster, but I think I can treat you to the Bistro's special—unless it's pork chops."

"You learn quick, John Stamey. I could turn you into a Reformed rabbi in no time." He stood, put on his coat and hat and I slipped on my U.S. Army surplus parka.

"That's what my father wants to make of me. The Christian equivalent, I mean."

"Ah, so your father wants you to join the family business and you want to go off with the French Foreign Legion, maybe?"

"Not quite that. What I really want to do is study anthropology. I took a minor in it and I can get a scholarship for my graduate work. But Dad has already pulled the strings and made arrangements for me to start seminary in Louisville, Kentucky." We went through the turnstile and stepped out into the bitter February wind. Those who speak of Tennessee's mild winters have never lived in Knoxville in the winter.

"The *real* question, young Mr. Stamey, is whether your disagreement is with your father or with God. It makes a difference you know."

"It's not with God. I don't believe in the literal translation of the Bible and I don't believe it's infallible like my father does, but I get along all right with God."

"So, you just don't want to be a professional preacher, John. Am I right?"

"You're right. I think maybe I'm a teacher, but I have no calling to be a pastor. Anthropology, now that *excites* me. I don't know why. And I also know that there aren't a lot of openings for professional anthropologists.

"Well, it was Pope who told us that the proper study of mankind is man. He was brilliant, that Alexander Pope. For a gentile."

We both laughed and walked, heads down against the bitter wind, without speaking again, to the Bistro on Gay Street. The Bistro shared space with the Bijou theater in one of Knoxville's most prized old buildings.

The special was a homemade chicken salad sandwich and we both ordered it, then sat warming ourselves over a mug of coffee. After a while, he broke the silence.

"You know, John, this thing between you and your father is nothing new. In Yiddish we have a saying: "*Red tsu der vand.*" It means, "Talk to the wall." Between fathers and sons, communication is almost always like talking to the wall."

"That's what Dad says," I replied with a smile.

"Let me tell you a story, John. I am full of stories, you know."

"I'm all ears, Rabbi."

"Once upon a time, there was a poor family in Berlin. The father was a devout rabbi, but a rabbi without a regular congregation. He was sort of like an itinerant Jewish preacher. He spent almost all his time at *shul*, studying and debating the fine points of law with other scholars.

Meanwhile, except for an occasional stint as a cantor or fill-in rabbi, his wife kept up the family doing menial labor. She began to call his time at *shul* a waste of time. 'You spend your days *shmoosing* with your friends," his wife would shout, "while I keep up the family. Some rabbi you are!"

The waitress brought our open-faced sandwiches with steamed vegetables on the side and Rabbi Goldstein stopped talking long enough to put his napkin in his lap and whisper a brief blessing.

He took a bite, chewed thoroughly with his eyes closed. "*This* is properly prepared," he said.

"But back to the story. The rabbi had a son. The boy loved his father, but he sided with his mother. Because his father brought in little income, the boy went to school in patched clothes and had to take charity, even for Hebrew studies.

Because the boy loved his father, he became very bitter with God. While he was at home, he went through the motions of going to synagogue, but he nourished a rage against his creator and vowed to one day have so much money that his fame would spread far and wide. Finally, he emigrated from Germany to America."

"Are you that boy?" I asked, a bite of chicken half-way to my mouth.

He stared at me for a moment through his smoky eyes in mock anger, then smiled. "Never interrupt a rabbi, John. It's bad luck—or it *should* be."

"Sorry," I said, "go on with your story."

"This boy," the white-haired rabbi continued, "he arrived in America with only a few dollars to his name. Soon he apprenticed himself to a tailor and spent years working for almost nothing. But one day he managed to buy his own shop. From there he got into manufacturing. Ten years after arriving in America, he was a millionaire. And, mind you, that was when a million was *real* money.

"Along the way, he had married a beautiful young woman. She gave him a son and almost died doing it. She could never carry another, so the rich man lavished everything on that one son. 'My boy,' he would boast to his friends, 'will someday run the empire I am building for him.'

"Then, one day when his son was ready to graduate from college, he came to his father with a shocking revelation. The boy was shaking so badly that it frightened the old man. 'Father, I have something to tell you,' he said.

"'So tell me. Don't beat around the bush! You know I hate that.' The old man thought his boy was about to confess to being gay or had fallen in love with a *shiksa*—that's a gentile girl."

'I'm not going to follow you in business,' the boy said in a trembling voice, 'I'm going to become an ordained rabbi.'

You wouldn't believe how the old man screamed and called his son everything from a *schmuck*, which is a very vulgar term in Yiddish, to *Reb Yankel*, which means an incredibly foolish man.

"The young scholar wouldn't budge, though. He went off to the seminary and became a rabbi. The whole time he was there, his father didn't speak to him or send him money.

"Then, on graduation day, the whole ceremony was interrupted by a man weeping in the audience. The young man turned and saw his father, a completely broken and repentant sinner. They were reunited that day and the old man once more became a good Jew. He spent a large part of his fortune after that for the up-building of his faith."

Rabbi Goldstein took a large bite of his sandwich and chewed it, seemingly in ecstasy, just as he had before.

"That's a very touching story," I said, sipping my coffee. Is your father still alive."

"No, my father died when I was three years old." He washed down the sandwich with coffee.

"Then *who* was the young man with the rich father?"

"Some guy I went to seminary with. I don't remember his name." He dismissed the thought with a casual wave of his hand. "Are you going to have dessert, John?"

Moments later, everyone in the Bistro was staring at me. I was laughing so hard that I had sucked coffee into my windpipe. The guffaws continued to boil up and overflow uncontrollably. And even as I laughed, I knew that I had made a decision and that I might never have made it without the man across the table from me.

"*Of course* we'll, have dessert, Rabbi. This is a celebration. I'm going to Boston to study anthropology."

"You see, John. Nothing is ever as bad as it seems," the rabbi said. "Here's another saying for you. I wouldn't be surprised if Mark Twain stole it from a rabbi. Mister Twain said, '*When we remember that we are all mad, the mysteries disappear and life stands explained.*'

"And if *that* thought doesn't get you through what's on your mind the next time, you can find me at the library almost every afternoon. "I think I'll have the cheesecake, John. How about you?"

It was twelve years before I went back to try and thank him for what he had done for me.

THE MAIN BRANCH of the Lawson McGhee Library hadn't changed much since I had left Knoxville, Tennessee far behind. I had been back for visits, of course, but only briefly. This time, with two weeks set aside for vacation, I had decided to revisit my past. Rabbi Jacob Goldstein was at the top of my list.

When I had left to pursue a graduate degree in anthropology, my father had been angry, even bitter. Strangely enough, though, my studies in anthropology eventually led me back to theology. In fact, among my degrees is a doctorate in religious studies.

Though I never returned to the doctrines inculcated in me at the Southern Baptist altar, my father made a practice of proudly telling his friends about his son, the Harvard Professor.

"Excuse me," I said to the young man with the ponytail who was behind the checkout counter. "I'm trying to locate a gentleman by the name of Goldstein. He's a rabbi and used to spend a lot of afternoons here. Maybe you remember his wool overcoat and black fedora."

I felt foolish. How many things can happen in twelve years and what were the odds he would still be wearing the same clothes?

"Not lately. How long ago was it?"

"About twelve years."

"Go up that spiral staircase and ask for Mrs. Tantor. She worked down here for years before going up to the research section."

I almost left, but found myself drawn upstairs by my desire to see Jacob Goldstein again, or at least find out what had happened to him. Mrs. Tantor was a pleasant woman in her early sixties with gray hair and round gold glasses. She listened politely to my description.

"A rabbi in a black wool coat, a fedora, and with white hair and smoky eyes. He was called Goldstein, you say?"

"Yes. Jacob Goldstein."

She sat for a moment, then smiled. "Would you wait just a minute."

I stood and looked around the familiar, yet unfamiliar scene until Mrs. Tantor returned with a manila folder. She opened it and handed it to me. I saw a glossy black and white 8x10 photo of a priest being led out of a church by two police officers. "Is this him?" she asked.

"It *looks* like Rabbi Goldstein, but the man in the picture is wearing a Roman collar."

"That was when he was Father O'Hara," the librarian said with a gentle smile. "Before that he was Reverend Bob Mitchell, a chaplain at Baptist Hospital. Once he even joined the Salvation Army, but he didn't bother to check with the hierarchy there either. He just promoted himself to Brigadier and started out to do good.

"His real name was Clarence Turner. He had been a brilliant lawyer before his wife died. Not long afterwards, though, he quit his job and went into the ministry—several, in fact. And without bothering to inform the people in charge.

"I don't really remember him as the rabbi, but this is obviously the man you're looking for."

"He was so wise and compassionate..." I began.

"Oh, yes. There was quite a stink when they found out who he really was and banned him from Baptist hospital. He had made the other chaplains look bad, I'm told."

"Do you know what happened to him?" I asked.

"I hate to be the bearer of bad news," she said softly, "but he died in jail about six years ago."

"How? Why..." Without warning I was too choked up to finish my sentence.

"As time passed," the librarian told me, "he became more and more convinced of his religious vocation. He began to go into churches, missions and synagogues and dispute with the real clergy. That's why he was being escorted out of the church in that picture.

"One evening, after he had been arrested for interrupting services at Church Street United Methodist Church, he died of a heart attack during the night, alone and in jail."

As I stood there, tears in my eyes, I suddenly flashed back to my lunch at the Bistro with Rabbi Jacob Goldstein. I smiled and shook my head ruefully.

"Are you all right?" Mrs. Tantor asked. "I'm *so* sorry you had to find out this way."

"I'm all right. I was just thinking about how much Rabbi Goldstein, or whatever what his name was, has meant to me through the years, and I just remembered something he attributed to Mark Twain."

"Would you share it with me?" she asked.

"Of course." I closed my eyes and reached back into memory. *"When we remember that we are all mad, the mysteries disappear and life stands explained."*

"How appropriate!" Mrs. Tantor actually clapped her hands in delight, like a character from a movie.

"Rabbi Goldstein—or whoever he really was—said Twain probably stole it from a rabbi. I wouldn't doubt that at all," I told Mrs. Tantor, "not even a little."

"Neither would I," she said. "Neither would I."

My Doe-eyed Southern Belle

THE FIRST TIME I saw Vickie Campbell at Dora's Grill the term "doe-eyed southern belle" popped into my mind. It's not something I would have said out loud, but I thought it.

She was a tiny woman—no more than five feet tall—who, at twenty-five, still had the appearance of a teenage girl. Her thick mane of glistening black hair tumbled down her back, in violation of health department rules, like a cascading waterfall. It was the kind of hair you only see in commercials about shampoo. Her skin was pale, almost translucent and her eyes were a startling light topaz blue, contrasting with her dark hair.

I was afraid she would run if I spoke too loudly or looked directly at her. So I ordered my breakfast, casting only covert glances at her trim figure and delicate ankles, shown off to good advantage by her snug, pink uniform. Dora insisted on the uniforms even though there were never more than three employees, counting her.

Eventually I became a regular at Dora's, but still maintained an aloof attitude towards Vickie. Not only did I fear scaring her away, but I hadn't asked a new female out since I was sixteen years old, three years before I married my childhood sweetheart.

The grill, a narrow building with a counter, a half dozen stools covered in cracked, red imitation leather and only two small matching tables, was Dora's hobby and passion. Her husband, a trucking executive supported her well enough. But after their only child, a tall blonde like Dora, married a carnival worker and moved to Florida, running the business kept her occupied. A few customers, like me, became surrogate children.

I always felt at home, which wasn't a bad feeling for a recently divorced man of twenty-nine who was pumping gas for a living, residing in a depressing one room apartment and writing magazine articles into the wee hours of the morning for an occasional small check.

Everyone knew that an ordinary customer had become a regular when Dora, an Amazonian-sized woman with a booming voice and blonde braids wrapped tightly around her head, yelled a greeting before the bell over the door stopped jingling.

"Two over easy with sausage and gravy," she'd yell as I entered. "The book writer is here." She called me that—even though I was years away from publishing my first book—because she had asked me about the *Writer's Market* I carried in one morning.

My acceptance as a regular came a month or so after I began to go in there; it was the morning I took my four-year-old in for a Saturday morning breakfast.

"And who might this lovely young lady be?" Dora asked in her loud voice with an Appalachian dialect that stood out even by the standards of rural Union County, her place of birth. Vickie, pouring coffee behind the counter, cast surreptitious glances at me and my daughter.

"My name is Celeste Michelle, but my friends call me Micki," my cotton-topped daughter piped up.

"You certainly talk well for such a little girl," Dora said, leaning forward over the counter.

"That's because my daddy never allowed anyone to talk baby—talk to me. He thinks it's silly."

"Well, he may be right about that, but he don't know beans about how to fix a little girl's hair. Take this child to the back and comb out the tangles, Vickie. And see if you can find a pink ribbon in my junk drawer."

Without hesitation, Vickie complied. Hardly anyone ever questioned Dora's orders. After about twenty minutes, they came back out. Micki's appearance had improved immensely.

"I got the tangles out," Vickie said in a small voice as she led Micki back by the hand. "She has pretty hair. Is her mother a blonde?" It was the first question she had ever asked me outside her professional capacity.

"You never know what color her mother's hair will be from week to week. The original color was a dark blonde when we were children."

"Childhood sweethearts," Dora boomed from behind the counter, leaning over on her elbows to look at me. "How long were you married?"

"Nine years."

"Why, you must have been hardly more than a child when you got married," Dora said.

"My mommy says Daddy is *still* a child," Micki said forthrightly. "She says his head has always been in the clouds and will never come down."

"Never you mind, Micki. A lot of great men have been dreamers," Dora told her.

"I was nineteen and she was seventeen when we got married," I said.

"You seem like the kind who *likes* marriage," Dora said thoughtfully, drawing a hard glance from Vickie, who was refilling my cup. I nodded noncommittally, though it ran through my mind that marriage was the one thing that I *never* wanted to try again, at least at that time of my life.

I forgot all about the conversation until a couple of weeks later. Meanwhile, I admired Vickie as she went about her duties, wondering if I'd ever recover enough self-esteem to ask her or any other woman out.

Though a child of the nineteen-sixties, I had missed the sexual revolution by virtue of a monogamous relationship throughout most of it. Even during my two years in the U.S. Army, I had remained faithful.

"MORNING," DORA SAID, "sliding into the chair across from me. The flimsy metal creaked under her weight. She wasn't fat, but she was a *big* woman.

"Good morning." I courteously put my *Knoxville News Sentinel* aside.

"How's little Micki?" she asked.

"She's getting used to the situation. At least she seems to be," I answered.

"Divorce is hard on a child," Dora said.

"Pretty hard on everybody," I answered. "Though my ex-wife got back into the dating scene pretty quick."

At that moment, Vickie brought my order to the table. She glanced pointedly at Dora while arranging my napkin and silverware. I had no idea what was passing between them, though I had learned by that time that Vickie spoke mostly with her eyes and with fluttering movements of her dainty hands.

"How's the service station business?" Dora asked when Vickie had gone.

"Dull, but it gives me a lot of free time to write."

"I wondered what a smart man like you was doing working at a gas station," Dora said.

"Well, I don't have a college education and there's nobody knocking my door down with a good job offer."

"You didn't come in yesterday. You weren't broke were you? I'd hate to think you missed breakfast because you were short of cash the day before payday. Your credit's good here, you know."

"I appreciate that, but I was just running a little late yesterday." The truth was, I had skipped *two* meals the day before because I had no money. Pride I had in abundance.

"I wanted to talk to you about something else," Dora finally said. "But go ahead and eat while your food's hot. You can listen while you chew."

Launching my attack on the over-easy eggs and sausage I soon had the yolks bleeding across the plate, just right to be soaked up by a large fluffy biscuit.

"I've noticed that you pay a lot of attention to Vickie," Dora said.

"She's very pleasant and pretty," I replied.

"I *knew* you thought she was pretty. I told her that, but she doesn't believe it. "

"I don't understand. Why *wouldn't* she believe it?" I asked, buttering and slathering a second biscuit with strawberry preserves.

"She's *real* shy. You wouldn't believe just how backward she is. The child hardly ever goes out."

"Why are you telling me this, Dora?"

"Well, you think Vickie's pretty, she thinks you're a real gentleman, and she just *adores* little Micki. She can't have any children of her own, you know. At least the doctor's don't advise it. She has a real bad case of Type I sugar diabetes."

I noticed that Vickie was casting frequent glances at us and that there was color in her cheeks. She seemed either angry or embarrassed; maybe both.

"Why don't you ask her out?" Dora finally asked.

"To be truthful, Dora," I paused and put my fork down. "I don't even remember *how* to ask for a date. I'm not the most outgoing person in the world."

"I *told* Vickie that's why you hadn't asked her out." Dora clapped her hands. "Do I know people or what?"

"I guess you do know people, Dora." I took a sip of coffee.

"So, the only reason you ain't asked her out is because you're too shy?"

"Yeah, kind of..." Vickie was staring directly at Dora, though she could not hear what we were saying above the voices of two or three people at the counter.

"Well, it just so happens, she's been *hopin'* you'd ask her out. So that settles that. I'll send her over to heat up your coffee and you can ask her."

"Wait..." I began, as Dora abruptly stood up and went behind the counter. There was a short, sharp exchange between Dora and Vickie behind the counter, but a moment later my doe-eyed Southern belle was standing by the table, refilling my cup.

"You don't *have* to ask me out," she said, in her tiny voice, eyes demurely lowered, long lashes fluttering. "Dora's too pushy sometimes. She thinks she's my second mother."

"I feel the same way. I mean, I don't want you to feel obligated, but the truth is, I've been too embarrassed to ask because it's been such a long time for me."

"I'm free on Sunday." Her cheeks flushed, but she looked directly at me for the first time.

"Sunday evening would be good." Suddenly I felt elated.

"Do you know where Mulberry Lane is?" she asked.

In 1974, even after several years of burned bras and vocal women with hairy legs and armpits, it was still generally understood, at least in Knoxville, Tennessee, that a man picked up a young woman at her door and paid for the evening's activities.

VICKIE CAMPBELL LIVED in the basement of a neat brick rancher owned by her parents in the north end of the county. Like a true

Southern gentleman, I went to the front door to be looked over by her parents, rather than going directly to the entrance she used.

Her father was a slight man who looked to be in his middle fifties, with a receding hairline and a barely perceptible paunch. When her mother entered the room, it was obvious where Vickie had gotten her delicate beauty. The mother simply looked like a slightly older and faded version of the daughter.

Both of them made me feel welcome, as if it was some kind of special occasion for Vickie to be going out. I wondered how they had raised such a beautiful daughter without getting used to admiring males.

When Vickie came up the stairs, she almost took my breath away. She was wearing her hair loose, except for mother-of-pearl combs on the sides, and a white peasant blouse that bared her shoulders and left her midriff uncovered, above loose white shorts. Young women of that era had all but stopped wearing bras and it was obvious to me that Vickie was following the trend. I hoped the wave of lust that had just rolled over me was not visible on my face.

"I'm ready when you are," she said, looking at me through lowered eyelids.

"Where will you be going?" her mother asked me, not in a prying manner, but by way of conversation.

"To a Mel Brooks film called *Blazing Saddles*, unless Vickie has someplace else she would rather go. I like Mel Brooks films."

"That sounds great," Vickie said. "I've heard it's a good movie."

"Have a good time," her father said as we went down the front steps. As I opened the car door for Vickie, I saw that they were still watching from the porch.

"Your parents seem nice," I said.

"They're all right," she answered.

The conversation consisted of short questions and comments from me and brief responses from her, all the way out to West Knoxville. Though the silence made me uncomfortable, I told myself that she was very shy and would need time to relax.

After refusing popcorn and all other refreshments—which I chalked up to her diabetes—Vickie sat stiffly through the movie, her delicate hands tightly gripping the arms of her seat, causing her knuckles to glow white in the light of the big screen. Occasionally, a smile would briefly cross her lips, but she never really joined in with the raucous laughter all around us.

Outside in the parking lot, I started my dilapidated Ford Maverick and let it run for a couple of minutes. Without warning, Vickie turned to me and said: "Would you mind if I smoked a little dope?"

The question caught me off-guard. I was no virgin when it came to marijuana, but I would have been willing to bet that she was. "No, go ahead," I told her.

To my surprise, she did not take out a rolled joint or a bag of marijuana. I instantly recognized the small dark lumps as hashish, marijuana's potent first cousin, gathered from the flowering tops of the hemp plant, mixed with oil and pressed into small cakes. Some said the harvesters got stark naked, oiled themselves down and ran through the fields collecting pollen, then scraped it from their bodies with sticks—but I had always considered it a doper legend.

I knew she was no beginner as she took out a small carved pipe,—a bong for which it is now a federal crime to own for the express purpose of smoking marijuana. Tommy Chong of Cheech and Chong fame went to the penitentiary for selling them on the Internet. Vickie fired up the hashish with a Zippo lighter and the acrid, unforgettable odor filled the car. After a couple of deep drags, she offered me the pipe.

"No thanks. Not while I'm driving," I said.

"Are you sure?" she asked. She took a deep breath, smiled and sort of squeezed her shoulders together as relaxation visibly spread through her entire body. It was as if I suddenly had another woman in the car with me.

She put away the paraphernalia, slid across the seat beside me and kissed me on the cheek. The nearness and the scent of her made me dizzy for a moment. A man living like a monk forgets how soft and fragrant women are.

"Want to get something to eat at Shoney's Big Boy," I asked. "It's the only place still open in North Knox County."

"Yeah, ain't Knoxville a *grand* city." she said, then leaned back, smiling to herself.

"Care for some music?" I asked.

"Sure," she said lazily.

I had the radio set for a rock and roll station and when I turned the ignition, the car was suddenly filled with the sound of the Eagles singing *Take It To The Limit.* By the time we had listened to tunes by John Lennon, The Grateful Dead, Simon and Garfunkel, The Who and Van Morrison, I was pulling off I-75 onto 25w at the Clinton Highway exit.

"Pull off somewhere. I want you to kiss me," Vickie said without warning.

It didn't take me long to find an unlit church parking lot. She flowed into my arms with the sensuous, sinewy movements of a house cat rubbing against your leg. Her lips were warm, wet and tasted of lipstick and hashish. I was hers for the taking, but after a few minutes, she sat up and pushed back her hair.

"We can save the rest for later," she said with a lascivious wink, while opening her purse to remove the pipe and hash again.

By that time *I* was so fired up that I probably would have kept silent if she had taken out a syringe and shot up heroin. My libido, which I had thought was in hiding, had emerged with a fury that shocked me. All I wanted to do was get through a quick meal and get her into bed. I was too excited to be ashamed of myself. My doe-eyed southern belle had turned into a vixen.

"Looks pretty busy," I said, pulling into a space at Shoney's a few minutes later.

"Just as long as I can get a piece of hot fudge cake. *Yum, yum!*" She licked her lips sensuously and closed her eyes. "Vanilla ice cream and whipped topping over that wonderful butter-grilled cake, all covered with hot fudge." She seemed to shiver in ecstasy.

"I thought…"

"Dora told you that I'm a diabetic, didn't she? Sometimes she's a *nosy old bitch*! I guess she also told you I'm not supposed to have kids and I'll go blind if I don't watch my diet. Well, *didn't* she?"

"No…Well, she did mention the diabetes," I admitted.

"Do you know how sick you can get of people feeling sorry for you? Do you know what it feels like to stick yourself four or five times every day and weigh every scrap of food?" She was becoming a little too strident, but I was still in the thrall of lust and missed the danger signs.

"I guess it's no fun at all," I responded. "You're a grown woman. I'd be the last person to butt into your business."

"Yeah, but you want to get *your* business into *my* butt, don't you?"

She had sat quietly through one of the funniest movies I had ever seen, without laughing. But she was giggling uncontrollably at her own wit as I pushed open the door and got out beside a seven-foot fiberglass statue of the "Big Boy".

As we went through the door, Vickie turned to me and smiled then spoke loudly enough for everyone within ten tables to hear. "What's the matter, Joey Savage? Are you shocked that poor, innocent little ol' Vickie has dirty thoughts?"

"Not shocked, just pleasantly surprised," I answered quietly as the waitress seated us, then took two orders for hot fudge cake, pretending not to hear what Vickie was saying, or that she was saying it so loudly.

After the waitress left, my doe-eyed southern belle-turned-vixen, sat quietly for a few minutes, looking around the room dreamily. I hoped that the mellowness of the hash would soon overtake her—as it should have already.

"Can you watch my purse while I go to the rest room?" she asked with a sweet smile.

"Sure," I replied. She made no move to get up, however. Instead, she continued to look around the room with a faraway expression. Two minutes or so passed before I said anything.

"Did you want me to watch your purse while you go to the rest room?" I quietly reminded her. It was a mistake on my part. Suddenly she was staring directly into my eyes and the rage almost made me recoil.

"*Do you think I need a man to tell me when to piss?*" she bellowed at a decibel level that could be heard all over the dining room. People turned to stare.

"No," I raised my hands to placate her. "You just said…"

"I *know* what I just said. All my life people have been standing over me. 'Vickie do this,' and 'Vickie do that.' It never seems to cross anybody's mind that maybe I *know* what I want."

"I didn't mean to upset you. I'm sorry."

"Poor baby," she cooed and smiled brightly. "I *know* you didn't mean to upset me. Be a dear and watch my purse while I go to the rest room."

While Vickie was gone, the waitress returned with our order and whispered to me. "The manager says if you can't get her to be quiet, you'll have to leave."

"I'm sorry. I've never seen her act this way." I squirmed uncomfortably, aware that our table had become the center of attention.

"What were you two whispering about?" Vickie demanded to know as she slid back into the booth.

"She just told me to enjoy my cake and I told her I would."

Taking a bite of the cake and ice cream, she closed her eyes, then swallowed. "My God! This is like having an orgasm," she said, her voice only slightly lower than before.

"It is good. Could you lower your voice a little, Vickie?"

"What's the matter. Is the big boy *embarrassed?*" she asked belligerently, her mood swinging wildly again.

"No. I just don't like sharing my affairs with other people. I'm a private person."

"Oh, *I see.* You don't want everybody here to know that you're trying to get in my panties." She giggled and took another large bite.

"Yeah. That's it."

"You men always think that women are numb from the waist down, don't you? My crotch throbs as hard as yours does when I'm hot. And don't tell me you didn't get a woody a while ago.

"Waitress!" she turned without warning in her seat, swinging that beautiful raven-colored hair over her shoulder. The breeze it created blew our paper napkins off the table. "Bring me a piece of strawberry pie—with extra whipped cream."

"Vickie, maybe you should stop now. I don't know much about…"

"That's right! You don't know jack-shit about *anything.* I want a piece of strawberry pie! *I want it now!*"

Her eyes were flashing like strobe lights in the darkness, but it was her dainty hands that told the real story of the rage boiling under her normally demure facade. Both her hands were relentlessly clenching and unclenching on the edge of the table, leaving her knuckles white, just as they had been at the theater.

"Excuse me…."

I looked up and saw a bald man in a white shirt and black tie standing by the table. "I'm the manager. I want you to pay your bill and leave before I have to call the police," he said quietly but firmly.

"You're throwing us out of this *dump?* I can't believe it," Vickie's voice grew louder and more grating with every word.

I picked up the check, took out a bill and handed it to the manager. "Keep the change," I said.

"Come on, Vickie." I took her by the arm, but she jerked it away. "You keep your fuckin' hands off me! I can walk by myself," she screamed. "Don't ever grab me again, stud. You got that?"

With the prickly dignity of an intoxicated person, she got up and walked towards the door, stopping to grab a handful of York Peppermint Patties from a bowl on the counter. I wondered how much of her behavior was from hash and how much was from a dangerously high blood sugar level. I knew almost nothing about the disease. I reached into my pocket to pay for the candy, but the manager waved me on. "Just get her out of here."

Outside, Vickie vented her rage on me. "What kind of a man are you?" she snarled, tossing her hair from side to side. "How could you let a two-bit restaurant manager throw us out of that chicken-shit place and not even argue?"

"Because you have hash in your purse and the police arrest people for that." I unlocked the car and opened the passenger side door for her.

"I think you were *afraid* of him," she said. "My hero. My big, fuckin' hero! You want this pussy, but you didn't say a word to defend me!" She tore off the foil wrapper and chewed up the first Peppermint Pattie, as I pulled the car onto the highway.

Watching her, I couldn't help but remember that the word *assassin* was derived from hashish because of a Muslim cult that had once given its members liquid hemp to drink before sending them out to slay the enemies of Allah.

"I *don't* want your pussy, Vickie. I just want to get you home!" I had never meant anything more in my life. The thought of having her go into a coma in my car while under the influence of hashish sent thrills of terror up my spine. Or worse, what if she died?

"Don't tell me *that*," she sneered. "Your pants were still bulging when we got to Shoney's." A tiny stream of chocolate ran down from the side of her mouth. She shoved in two more pieces of candy and chewed them defiantly.

"For some strange reason, the mood has passed!" I focused my eyes on the road as I took the northbound ramp of I-75.

"Well, I can take care of that." She swallowed the mouthful of candy, pulled the blouse over her head and thrust two beautiful pear-shaped breasts towards me. What I had fantasized about for months was suddenly before my eyes in the flesh.

"Did that do it, or do you need more? How about *this*?" She raised her hips and slipped out of her shorts and panties, leaving her clad only in white sneakers.

For the briefest moment, lust reasserted itself and I had the insane urge to pull over by the side of the interstate and make love to her without preliminaries. Then reason prevailed. I had no desire to be checked out by a curious lawman. Not with a beautiful naked woman in my car, wearing white sneakers and carrying hash in her purse. Besides, I prefer my lovers awake.

"Feel'em Joey." She grabbed my right hand and pulled it to her chest. "Aren't they smooth. Don'tcha want a taste? Come on. Jus' a *little* taste."

Vickie was growing lethargic and her words had begun to slur, which I suspected was the result of diabetes and not hash. By the time I pulled over to the side of the road in an empty campground, a mile from her house, she was almost unconscious.

Getting the blouse back on was a lot easier than the shorts and panties. But I managed. As distressed as I was, her body under my hands as I dressed her, caused my backed up libido to scream for relief. But I only looked. A gentleman does not take advantage.

"You're no fun at all," she mumbled as I supported her to the door of her apartment and held her up while I searched through her purse for the door key.

Finally inside, I helped her lie down on the bed. I was torn between leaving and waking her parents to tell them what she had done; the part about the cake and candy, anyway.

I was saved from my dilemma when her mother, hair in pink curlers and wearing a blue terry-cloth robe, opened the stairway door and turned on the light.

"I...That is, Vickie ate some sweets and...." I felt like a child caught playing doctor.

"It's not your fault," her mother said quietly. "She promised not to do it again. But, as usual, she didn't keep her word." I didn't know if she was talking about drugs or sugar or taking her clothes off in my car, so I didn't say anything.

"Goodnight," Mrs. Campbell said. "I'm sorry your evening ended this way. You seem like a nice young man."

Uttering some sort of inane comment, I backed up and opened the door. As I left, Vickie's mother was leaning over her. A minute later,

I was hurtling down the interstate, putting distance between us. My first new date since adolescence had been a disaster.

I wondered if I would ever be able to look Vickie Campbell in the eyes again without thinking of pear-shaped breasts and a tiny waist flaring into soft creamy hips and a pubic area with hair so fine and silky as to look almost bare. I was only human.

It was going to be a long night. I knew that for sure. Deciding between extreme embarrassment and a cozy, familiar breakfast place where I could get food on credit was not a decision to be made lightly by a divorced man living on minimum wage while writing the great American novel.

Too Good to Be True

"THERE WON'T BE an open casket at Sergeant Free's funeral," the young man who had been the first officer on the scene said. He was tall and angular with freckles and red hair. He looked like he was trying not to throw up. "That was *some* explosion. Whoever wired it knew what he was doing."

The stench of blood permeated the scorched air. Most people don't even know that blood has a smell. It does, though—an indescribable, yet unforgettable odor.

"Fortunately, he had already made arrangements to be cremated," I told the young cop.

"Lieutenant, if Sergeant Free was a friend of yours...I wasn't trying to be flip. I used to work for him. He was the best boss I ever had since I've been on the streets," the young cop said.

"We *were* friends—eighteen years, this month—but I took no offense at what you said and it wouldn't have offended Jack, either. He always said *exactly* what he meant."

He stared at me from the corner of his eye, trying not to be obvious about it. He was probably wondering how I could sound so detached when the mutilated remains of my best friend were lying twenty feet away, covered with a sheet. He obviously hadn't been a cop long enough to perfect *his* mask.

"You haven't let anyone inside the crime scene, have you?"

"No, Lieutenant Cooper. Of course not." He sounded hurt. "Well, the guy from the bomb squad is in there looking around, but he said you wouldn't mind."

"No problem," I told him. "He knows what he's doing, but we don't want *anybody* else near here until the crime scene technicians are finished. And don't forget to log everyone who enters the crime scene—and that includes the Chief of Police—if he's sober and decides to be on television today."

"Sergeant Free's cruiser is still running, Lieutenant." The patrol officer said. "I found his keys on the sidewalk. The explosion blew them all the way out here." He handed me the key-ring. It was stained with Jack's blood, already dried. I didn't mention to the young cop that he had taken something from a crime scene because there had been no damage done and because I was just as rattled as he was the first time I saw the mutilated body of someone I knew.

"Fill me in," I said, signaling another nearby uniform to take the log sheet.

As we walked towards Jack's cruiser, I worked hard to stay dispassionate. In eighteen years as a cop in Knoxville, Tennessee, I have learned to let *nothing* show on my face. Not even the pain of losing a man who was as close as any brother could have ever been.

The cruiser was running, just as the patrolman had said, but the door was locked. A good cop never forgets to lock the door, and Jack was as good as they come.

"Call went out as a second party, 'person in distress.' Sergeant Free said he'd take it because he was close. He notified dispatch that he'd arrived, then walked up on the porch. Dispatch says he keyed the radio and they heard the explosion before the radio went dead. Guy across the street saw it. I told him not to leave the house until you talked to him."

I unlocked the door to Jack's cruiser and got in. The inside was neat, just like his cruiser had always been neat when he was breaking in a new rookie named David Cooper. Jack Free had taught me everything I needed to be a good cop. That was eighteen years ago. I eventually moved on to burglary and larceny, then homicide, but Jack loved the streets too much to take off his blue suit.

Patrol had changed a lot since I left. The video camera with its blinking lights was one of the new innovations and laptop computers right in the cruiser for officers to run their own checks. I reached out and punched a button that said "rewind." There was a whirring sound, then a click. I touched the "play" button and a picture flickered on the 4 inch monitor mounted in the dash. I leaned forward with interest. The date and time imprinted on the video tape indicated that Jack had stopped the vehicle less than two hours earlier.

"If these recorders can be run back at will, what keeps officers from erasing what they don't want anyone to see?"

"Only supervisors can disable the rewind lock and change the tapes. I guess Sergeant Free forgot to lock his back down when he changed the tape at the beginning of the shift," the patrol officer said.

Squinting at the small screen, I recognized the tall, thin, black man getting out of the Cadillac stopped in front of Jack's cruiser. It was Johnny Blaine, a thug and drug dealer Jack and I had tried unsuccessfully to take down for the five years we were together on the beat. Apparently Jack had still been after him—right up until a few two hours before his death.

"Just Plain" Blaine had been responsible for at least a half dozen murders and most of the dope that went to school children all over the city. Jack despised Blaine. We knew he had sold the crack cocaine and marijuana laced with angel dust to a ninth grader, right before boy killed both his parents and wounded a police officer. But *knowing* and *proving* are not the same.

Blaine had always proven to be too slick for us, though, and had the best lawyers money could buy. He had never been convicted of *anything* and his continued existence on Earth as a free man highly offended Sergeant Jack Free.

"Lieutenant, you can turn on the sound with that knob on the left side of the little monitor," the patrol officer said. I turned up the volume and listened. Blaine was speaking, but his voice sounded hollow and tinny.

"How come you always stoppin' me for no reason. This is *twice* in a week, now. You shoulda learned after all these years that you can't take down old Blaine.' The drug dealer smiled arrogantly, teeth ivory white in his brown face. He pushed the white Panama that he was wearing back on his head.

"You're *always* doing something wrong, Blaine. But I want to talk to you about something I heard you've said—about *me*."

I tried not to let the patrol officer see that I was choking up, watching Jack Free alive and well, just a couple of hours earlier, all stocky shoulders and glistening gun-leather. Though much shorter than the drug dealer, he commanded the situation with his presence. Suddenly, what Jack was saying on the video-audio had my attention, though.

"I hear you're bragging around town that you intend to do me in or have someone do it for you. What do you say about that, Blaine?" Jack Free asked.

"Why thas' a *absolute* lie. Tell me, who said I was gonna hurt you? *Who said that?*" Blaine sounded genuinely outraged, a perfect figure of a man unjustly accused. But that's how he's stayed out of jail all these years. He knows how to play the game.

"Never mind *who* said it. Just be aware that I *know* about it," Jack told him. "It'll take more than a punk like you to end my career. Anyway, *if* you pulled it off, you'd find out how many cops there are in Knox County."

The drug dealer was still waving his long skinny arms and shouting his absolute innocence when Jack pulled away. That was how my old partner was—straight to the point. I ran the tape back again and jotted down the tag number of the Cadillac Blaine had been driving. I added some additional information and handed it to the young patrol officer.

"Have dispatch *BOLO* this information immediately. The driver will be Johnny Blaine, also known as 'Just Plain' Blaine. Any unit making contact should use caution because he's my prime suspect in the homicide of a police officer. When he's located, I want him held at the scene until I arrive."

As I turned from the car, the bomb squad man came down from the heap of smoking rubble where a small house had stood between two vacant lots. He was looking at some fragments of metal in the palm of his hand. I've always wondered if the explosive experts always seem so calm because they refuse to think about what they're handling or because they're crazy. I recognized the short, stocky man in black coveralls as Eddie Travis, another old comrade from patrol.

"What can you tell me off the top of your head, Eddie?"

"Well, it was plastic explosive and whoever set it had done his homework. It was almost surgical. Just enough to take this little house down and kill whoever was on the porch, but not enough to even blow the windows out across the street.

"The guy across the street says Jack didn't touch the door," Travis went on, "so I figure the explosion was detonated from a distance."

"Why?"

"Because the *timing* was too good. That bomb went off as soon as Jack got to the door. Whoever set this up couldn't have known *exactly* when Jack was going to walk up to the door. I can't be sure about any of this yet, but that's my gut reaction.

"Of course, it's within the realm of possibility that it was a coincidence or that there was a switch set to go off when someone sent vibrations through the porch by walking on it—but I doubt it. I think you should look for a remote device until I tell you otherwise."

At that moment the radio crackled out my call number.

"Go ahead, dispatch." I said.

"Lieutenant, patrol has found the Cadillac and the suspect you were looking for. They have him in custody at his residence, one block south of you, at 2322 Willow Street. Be advised that the original call on which Sergeant Free was dispatched came in from a pay phone across the street from that address."

"That didn't take long," Eddie said.

I stood quietly for a moment. "Eddie, would a detonator work from a block away?"

"Sure," he shrugged. "Some from a lot further away than that. Whoever used the detonator, though, had to be able to see Jack walk up on the porch, or at least have been in contact with someone who could see him."

JOHNNY BLAINE WAS standing between two husky patrol officers, his left eye swollen, when I arrived. He had apparently not been cooperative. Neither of the officers looked happy. They both were men who had been trained by and had worked for Sergeant Jack Free, and you didn't work for him without learning to love and respect him. He was that kind of man.

"Offisuh Cooper," Blaine shouted almost hysterically as I got out of the car. "These men sayin' I had somethin' to do with killin' Jack Free. Tell'em it ain't so. I *respected* Jack Free. You know that!"

"Then you won't care if I look in your car, will you, Blaine?"

"No. Go right ahead. I didn't kill no cop. I been in the house all day. I swear to God I ain't been outta the house." The videotape in Jack's car, of course, said differently.

"Take the cuffs off and let him sign a 'consent to search form,'" I told the officers. They reluctantly took the cuffs off just long enough for him to sign the form, then clamped them back on. As soon as the consent form was in my hands, I opened the door of the Cadillac.

It took me about 30 seconds to find what I was looking for. It was hidden wedged between the door post and the front seat—a small black, plastic case with a silver button and a small antenna at the top.

I don't know much about electronics, but I had no doubt what I was holding.

I slowly walked across the street to the phone booth and looked north. The smoldering site where Jack Free had died was clearly visible, across several vacant lots, from the phone booth. I went back to where Blaine was standing between the two patrolmen, and took out a small card I carry for just such occasions.

"Mister Blaine, you have the right to remain silent. If you give up the right to remain silent…"

"You've done a good job, Lieutenant," Chief of Detectives Fraker wheezed, rolling a cigar stub around in his mouth. There was a no smoking policy in the detective bureau and he had instituted it, but never complied himself. The shirt he was wearing was freshly washed, but the front was covered with cigar ashes. One day his heart would stop, because of his 300 pound bulk and the cigars he constantly smoked, inhaling them until the hot ash was close enough to burn his fingers.

"I really didn't do much, Chief. It all fell together. We had the videotape, the phone number across the street from Blaine's house and the transmitter. Of course, the bomb people can't tell us if the transmitter was the same frequency as the one used to detonate the bomb."

"I don't think a jury is going to quibble over a little detail like that, especially when they find out that the house where the bomb killed Jack was rented in Blaine's name," the chief said, "don't forget *that*."

"Yeah, but the rental people never met whoever rented the house. It was all done by phone."

The chief leaned back in his soft leather chair and sighed. *"Hells bells, Cooper!* If somebody gave you a million dollars on a platter you wouldn't be happy. Let's have it. What's eating you?"

"Something that Jack Free taught me when I was a rookie. He always said that if a thing *looks* too good to be true, then it *is* too good to be true. This case is too good to be true," I told the chief.

"What's the motive?" I continued before he could interrupt me. "We've been on Blaine's case for years and nothing like this happened before. He's always depended on his money and his lawyers. Why didn't Blaine try to cover his trail? He's a low-life but isn't stupid. This entire case *feels* wrong."

"I think you're having a delayed reaction to the loss of a friend," Fraker said. "You've got enough evidence to hang this low-life, murdering, cop-killing, sonofabitch. *Be happy.* Go home and get some rest."

"Guess I will, Chief. I'm tired."

"Before you leave, though, stop and talk to Sergeant Sweet. He says it's important."

"What have I done this time to bring myself to the attention of Internal Affairs? Did I forget to say 'please" and "thank-you" to some dirt-bag, or have I parked in a no parking zone somewhere?"

"Give it a rest, Dave." The chief of detectives fired up his lighter and relit his cigar stub. "The head-hunters have a job just like we do."

I left the chief's office, muttering under my breath and stopped just down the hall in front of the door with an inscription on a brass name plate that said "Internal Affairs." I knocked.

"Come in," Sergeant Sweet said from behind the door.

Sergeant Sweet is the only living human being I know who actually qualifies for the term "cadaverous." In addition to his sickly appearance, he has a bad twitch in his left eye and a habit of running his fingers around his collar as if it's choking him, even though it barely touches his turkey gobbler neck. He left the streets after 5 years to investigate other cops. Internal affairs officers have their place, I guess. But so do vultures and maggots.

"What's the new complaint, Sergeant?" I asked without preliminaries. "Did somebody see me in public without a tie?"

"Close the door, Lieutenant. Let's just skip the insults today. This is important. It probably has something to do with Jack Free's murder."

That got my attention. I sat down and waited as Sweet went through a folder. He finally found what he was looking for and removed two separate reports.

"This," Sweet said, holding up two sheets of paper, "is a complaint from a street dealer by the name of Chi Chi Sandoval who says that Jack Free stopped him one night and shook him down for a large quantity of hydrocodone."

I was almost out of my seat when Sweet snapped at me. "Sit down! I'm not here to assassinate Jack Free's reputation. But you *need* to know this." Sweet tugged at his collar, staring angrily at me. "I'm still a cop, whether you believe it or not. I closed this file as *unfounded* over four months ago. It was the dealer's word against Jack's." Sweet pitched the other report on the desk in front of me.

"*This* case is still open, though—or it was until Jack bought the farm this morning. A patrol officer noticed that there was a discrepancy in the number of pills he seized from a dealer and what his Sergeant, Jack Free, turned in. The patrolman thought he'd made a serious counting error. He didn't even *suggest* that Jack had taken the pills—but he didn't know about this other file, either."

"So what are you going to do now?" I asked.

"I'm going to disappear the file. Jack's out of my jurisdiction now. I just thought the information might help *your* investigation."

The tears almost got over the rims of my eyes. Sweet looked away until I could compose myself. *Jack Free involved in drugs?* Had a man who dedicated his life to eradicating the human filth who peddled dope to kids have been involved in drug trafficking? It was about to overwhelm me. Finally, I managed to choke out a "thank you" to Sergeant Sweet.

"You're welcome, Lieutenant Cooper. He tugged at his collar and I saw what looked almost like tears glistening in *his* eyes.

The sun had gone down and the night people—whores, pimps, fruit-hustlers, drug-dealers and small-time thugs—were hitting the streets, nocturnal creatures drawn like moths to the flashing neon lights of our local version of the red-light district. I waited, parked in an alley, still stunned from what Sergeant Sweet had told me. I *had* to know the whole truth, even if it was something that would muddy my memory of Jack Free. Sleep and rest would wait until I had found out what I needed to know.

I didn't have to wait long. A slight, mousy man with a receding hairline stepped from one of the many peeling doorways in the old apartment house across the street. He looked both ways, up and down the sidewalk, caution born of the kind of world which he inhabited. His street name was Zorro. I never knew why he was called that and I had long ago forgotten his real name, but if anybody knew about Jack, he would. Their relationship as cop and snitch went back a long way.

Quietly, I got out of the car and crossed the street. I was almost on him before he saw me. His eyes darted here and there and his muscles flexed for flight.

"Don't run, Zorro! If you do, I'll lock you up and you'll never score your black tar heroin tonight. *Think about it.* I just need to talk."

He relaxed, then turned and walked into the shadow of a building. I knew he was praying that none of his friends would see us talking.

"I heard about Sergeant Jack. Sorry to hear it, man. He was always good to me. And I know you two were friends from way back." Zorro's skin was fish-belly white with little veins showing through. I doubted if he had seen the sun in years.

"That's what I need to talk to you about, Zorro. I hear Jack was into painkillers and maybe that's why he's dead."

"Come on, Lieutenant, don't ask me questions about Sergeant Jack. He's gone and nobody's perfect. Let his memory alone."

"You *have* to tell me what you know, Zorro. I won't let go until you do. I'm sorry, but that's the way it is."

"When my sister died," Zorro said, choking back a sob, "Sergeant Jack got me outta jail and bought me a suit for the funeral. He treated me like a *human being.* Don't ask me to talk bad about him. *Please* don't do it." He dropped his eyes.

"He was *my* friend long before you met him, Zorro. I *have* to know why he's dead or I'll never be able to rest again. And you have to tell me what you know. Was Jack stepping into somebody's profit margin?"

"All right." The emaciated little man sighed. "Word on the street is that Sergeant Jack has been scoring some heavy drugs the last few months—ripping off street dealers. I didn't want to believe it at first, but then it began to come to me through good sources."

"What kind of drugs? Heroin? Cocaine? "

"Naw, just pills. Heavy pills, though. At first, it was just codeine-based stuff. Then he kicked it up to heavier stuff with a morphine base—Demerol, Oxycotin and Dilaudid. It's been going on for a while. I asked him about it as soon as I heard. He told me not to worry about it, that everything was cool."

"What was he doing with them?"

"I don't know, Officer Cooper. Honest to God! I ain't heard nothing' about how he was disposing of them. Can I go?"

"Are you telling me everything you know, Zorro? If you aren't, I'll be back and you're not hard to find."

"It's, the truth, man. That's all I know."

"Get out of here then—and thanks, Zorro."

He nodded, put his hands in his pockets, looked up and down the street and set off in search of his god and salvation. I watched him out of sight, then went back to my car.

There was one other place where I could find answers tonight. It wasn't something I wanted to do, but I had to know.

"DAVE, COME IN. I've been waiting for you."

Carol Free's face showed the strain of what had happened early in the day. She was in control, though. At 39, with auburn colored hair and freckles across the bridge of her nose, she still could have passed for a woman in her twenties. She was often mistaken for Jack's daughter, especially after the gray began to streak his hair.

"I would have been here earlier..."

"You don't have to explain, Dave." She kissed me on the cheek. "You were out trying to catch the people responsible for killing my husband and your best friend. Jack would have done the same."

"I need to ask you some questions?"

"I know," she nodded. "Do you have any suspects? They didn't say much on the evening news, and the chaplain didn't have any details."

"I probably have Jack's killer in custody. A drug dealer by the name of Blaine. I'm trying to wrap up some loose ends, though. It may have had something to do with a case Jack was on."

"I understand. Let's sit down. Bobby's asleep. The doctor gave him a sedative. I waited up because I knew you'd be coming."

"How *is* Bobby?"

"The image of his father. He starts college in the spring, you know."

"Doesn't seem long since we took him fishing the first time," I said. "I remember that Jack and I surprised him with a rod and reel when he was twelve. We..."

Suddenly, the tears that I had not shed earlier for my best friend were there, running down my face. I should have been comforting Carol, but she let me sob quietly on her shoulder. I've had two wives, and I wouldn't have cried in front of either of them. Carol is a special woman.

When I was under control again, she went into the kitchen and came back with a glass of peach brandy. Neither Jack nor I had ever been heavy drinkers, but we used to sit and sip cheap brandy sometimes. I took a big swallow and the slow burn in my belly felt good.

"Can you tell me if there's been anything different about Jack during the last few months?"

"Yes." She didn't hesitate, as if she had been wanting to discuss it with someone for a while. "He was withdrawn and preoccupied. And he was spending a lot of time in his little office workshop."

"He's always spent time down there tinkering with stuff from the electronics store, Carol. What was different?"

"It's hard to say, exactly. It was like he was working on a deadline for the last few months. He was carrying in a lot of technical manuals and magazines, and being secretive about them."

"What kind of manuals?"

"I don't know. Some were like the kind you get from the government. But I never really saw them close up. He kept them locked in a cabinet. He didn't hide the key or anything. It was right there on his desk, but I knew he didn't want me to look at them, so I didn't."

"Maybe we'd better take a look at them now," I said.

"I'm afraid not. I opened the cabinet this afternoon and it's empty. Whatever technical manuals he had in there, he's disposed of them."

"Why did you decide to look at them today, Carol?"

"Because," a sob caught in her throat, "I've known for months that something was wrong, and that whatever it was had to do with the project he had going on down there. You can't love a man like I loved Jack Free and not know when something is badly wrong. I just didn't know *what*—and I still don't. Damn it, David. My husband's dead! What was going on? Do you have any idea?"

"No," I lied to her for the first time since we had met eighteen years before, "but I need to look through Jack's files. There may be some clues, a place to start." There was no need to mention the internal affairs investigations or the drugs. Whatever *I* learned, Carol and Jack's son Bobby deserved good memories. I didn't know what I'd tell her when I did find out the truth.

CAROL FREE OPENED her husband's little office and workshop for me and went to bed. The room reflected his passion for orderliness. Aside from the personal computer and the television and video player, I knew very little about the gadgets around the room.

I don't know a lot about computers, but Jack nagged me into buying one a couple of years ago and showed me the basics. I knew that his files would be on disks, because his orderly mind would be satisfied with nothing less than complete back up of everything on the hard drive. I turned on the computer and a menu appeared.

I clicked on the icon for the program where I figured his personal documents would most likely be stored and told the computer to list them. Sure enough, they were there, all neatly categorized in a subdirectory called PERSONAL. I began to scroll through them, not sure what I was looking for, but knowing that my answers would be there somewhere.

I scrolled through and watched the document names move from the bottom of the screen upwards. OPEN CASES, CLOSED CASES, GRAND JURY, INSURANCE, CAR EXPENSES, MORTGAGE, COLLEGE FUND, then, without warning, COOPER.

Jack had left a file for me! I moved the cursor down the screen to the file and clicked. There was a beep and ENTER PASSWORD appeared on the screen.

Leaning back in the chair, I reached for a cigarette, then reminded myself that I had quit smoking a year ago. Since Jack had left a file for me, he would have kept the password simple. It would be something we had in common, something he would expect me to remember.

I tried the obvious first by typing in DAVID, then DAVID C. Both times the screen said ACCESS DENIED. *No big deal,* I thought, *if he had made it too easy, anyone who knew my name could have accessed the file.* The password would be something that Jack and I had in common, but something which wouldn't occur to anyone else unless they knew us well.

I typed in 2DELTA12, which was our car number when Jack was training me. ACCESS DENIED once more appeared on the screen. I left off the 2 and tried DELTA 12, then DELTA by itself, but with no luck.

Smiling to myself at overlooking the most obvious, I typed in my badge number, 1421, with confidence. ACCESS DENIED. Jack's badge number didn't work either. It was going to be more difficult than I thought.

An hour later, I had tried a hundred combinations, everything from my initials to mine and Jack's birthdays and astrological signs. Nothing worked. The screen kept reading out, ACCESS DENIED. I sat back with a frustrated sigh to consider my alternatives.

The possible combinations of numbers and letters were practically infinite. There were people at the department, I knew, who could break a password with relative ease, using computer forensics programs. I also knew that Jack Free would have built enough safeguards into *his* program to prevent snooping. If anyone tried to break the code from outside, they would end up with an erased disk. It looked like a dead-end.

It had been too much to hope that Jack Free had left the answer to his puzzle for me to find. It was just wishful thinking. The file with my name was probably *about* me. It had looked *so* obvious, though, just like the kind of puzzle Jack would leave.

Oh well, I thought to myself, getting up from the chair, *like Jack always said, if it looks too good to be true, then it is too good to be true.* I paused for a moment, then sat back down.

Slowly and deliberately, I began to type T-O-O-G-O-O-D. The computer whirred softly and the screen lit up.

CONGRATULATIONS DAVID!

The bottom shelf of the bookcase behind
you lifts out. Even Carol doesn't know
about it. Inside the false bottom you
will find a DVD and pistol.
The pistol is yours. I meant to give it
to you on your next birthday, but I won't
be there. Play the DVD to find your
answers. P.S. Made you work for it,
didn't I?

The pistol was a Glock 26 with my name engraved on the barrel. Jack and I had looked at pistols together a few weeks earlier and he knew I was planning on buying one when I had a little extra cash. The DVD had no label. My eyes were moist as I fed it into the computer's CD ROM slot. There was a flicker of the screen and Jack was looking at me with that wry grin of his.

"I had faith in you, David. I knew you wouldn't accept the obvious because it was too good to be true. You have a lot of questions, so let's get too it.

"This drama began four months ago when I began to have some bad headaches and double vision. I told Carol I was going to Atlanta for a patrol supervisor's seminar. I suspected there was something badly wrong, so I had my headaches checked out by a doctor there because I didn't want to worry Carol unnecessarily, if it turned out to be nothing.

"But, as we say in the police business, it was a worse case scenario. The tumor was already inoperable. The doctor gave me six months at most, with the last two to be lived in agony. He gave me a prescription for the pain and told me to see a doctor at home.

"When it came down to it, Dave, I *really* wasn't really afraid of death." Jack stopped long enough to light a cigarette, then smiled. "Yeah, I've started smoking again. There didn't seem to be much reason to deny myself.

"Anyway, I wasn't afraid of death, but there were a few things bothering me. Even with my insurance, Carol was going to be a little short on Bobby's college tuition. If I could die in the line of duty, though, I knew she'd get the extra money from Uncle Sugar. Also, I knew that if I spent my last two months in the hospital, the bills would eat up a lot of money. The thing that bothered me most, though, was that Carol and Bobby—and you—would have had to watch me go from bad to worse, and maybe eventually have to decide whether to pull the plug.

"And it bothered me a lot that Johnny Blaine was going to be the winner in our twenty year battle. After I was gone, he'd still be peddling drugs to kids and killing people for money."

Jack stopped again, opened a small bottle, shook two pills into his hand and washed them down with what looked like brandy straight from the bottle. "You'll have to excuse me, Dave. The pain really is excruciating.

"That's why I've been shaking down the drug dealers. Hey, do I know you or *what?* I knew you'd find out about the shake-downs and missing pills, and I knew you wouldn't just let it go to make it easier on yourself. But I needed enough painkiller to see my project through, and I couldn't see a doctor here. I figure the good I've done in my life will balance out a few pills ripped off from criminals.

"I had four months, at most, to get ready before the pain became unbearable. Most of the electronics expertise, I already had. The hardest part was learning how to make a precision bomb. I could have manufactured everything I needed from a few government manuals and *The Anarchist's Cookbook*—including the plastic explosives.

"Fortunately I didn't have to. There was C-4 that the bomb squad had seized, stored out at the range. Opening the safe was child's play. I traded some ordinary play dough for what I needed. One day they may find out that some of it is missing—but they won't tell anybody because they'd have to explain where it went.

"The *hard* part was keeping it from Carol. She knew something was wrong, but I couldn't tell her.

"I rented the little house through the mail because it was on a lot by itself and there wasn't much chance of hurting anyone else—and because it could be seen from the phone booth across from Blaine's house.

"Once I was ready, all I had to do was connect Blaine to the crime scene. You may have noticed on the tape you saw, he mentioned that I had stopped him *twice* this week. It was the first stop when I planted the detonator.

"I had already picked the time and date. All I had to do was punch that date into the video camera in my cruiser before I stopped him the last time. People accept as gospel the time and dates on a videotape tape.

"You already know the rest. At just the right time, I made the call across from Blaine's house. Then I told dispatch I was close. Just in case, though, I had sent the regular beat car on an errand so he wouldn't show up.

"The master touch—if I do say so myself—was how I detonated the bomb. I matched the frequency on the detonator to the frequency of my portable radio. As you know by now, since you are watching this video, I walked up on the porch and called dispatch to let them know I had arrived. When I keyed the radio, it set off the bomb. Hopefully, nobody was injured but me. I was pretty careful.

"Neat job, huh?" Jack Free smiled at me again. "Of course, I knew you'd never accept it at face value, especially after you found out about the pills. So I left you this little trail, with complete confidence that you'd figure it out. I didn't want you to spend the rest of your life thinking I had gone bad—and I guess I wanted to share my last bust with you.

"Of course, I also knew you'd feel compelled to turn this DVD over to the attorney general because you're such a boy scout, Dave. I made sure you didn't have to make that decision. Even as you watch it, this disk is being erased. Nobody else will ever see it. Ditto for the computer file, it was to be viewed only once. You'd look pretty silly trying to prove that 'Just Plain' Blaine didn't kill me when all the *evidence* says he did.

"Yeah, I *know*. The DVD and the file from my hard drive can be restored with the right technology. But I hope after you think this through, you'll respect my wishes. It's the last time you'll ever have to cover my back, and I've got a lot riding on it.

"I spent my entire adult life, old friend, looking for a thing called justice. Blaine didn't kill *me*, but he killed six or eight others that I personally know of—and got away with it—not counting the kids he's poisoned with crack cocaine, meth and PCP. And I *have* died in the line of duty, old friend. I think the term, *poetic justice*, applies to this situation.

"Tomorrow's the day for me. I'm glad it's almost over. I couldn't have kept it hidden much longer. I'd tell you take care of Carol and Bobby, but I know you'll do that anyway." He smiled for the last time. "I always knew you loved Carol as much as I did but would have died rather than admit it.

"Take it easy, see how things go. There may be a future for the two of you. She loves you too. If it happens, don't pass it up because we were friends and it might conflict with that Boy Scout oath you once took. If it works out, the two of you have my blessing.

"That's about it. I'm going to drink some more brandy and try to get through the last night of my life, Adiós, old friend. Remember, if it *looks* too good to be true, then it *is*." Jack Free reached forward and turned off the video camera.

For a few minutes I sat quietly, letting the tears go, then I took out the erased DVD, got a pair of pliers from Jack's work bench and broke it into small pieces. I put them in my coat pocket until I could toss them in the Tennessee River on my way home. Jack Free's last case had been closed and I would not reopen it.

Cop's lose most of their battles. Before we decided that we liked Saint Michael the Archangel, patron of warriors better, the cops' saint was Jude, the patron of lost causes. But Jack had won his last battle.

I raised the glass of peach brandy Carol had poured for me in a final toast to Jack, swallowed it in one gulp and once again felt the slow burn as it went down.

Kill the Dragon, Drink Its Blood

THE DRAGON LURKS on US Highway 129, a stretch of road on the Tennessee side of the Smoky Mountains, waiting to take the unwary. Ethan Dieumegard was on his way to kill that dragon and drink its blood.

Most serious motorcycle riders in America know about the Dragon. Ethan was not really a serious motorcycle rider and had never heard of the Dragon until three months earlier. He was on his way from Nashville to kill the Dragon and drink its blood because his fiancée had left him for an adventurer, a man of lesser intellect, and Ethan had a point to make, though he wasn't quite sure what it was.

Some say the Dragon starts at Robbinsville, North Carolina and runs fourteen miles over into Tennessee, where it ends at Tabcat Bridge in Blount County. Those who say that are wrong. The *real* dragon, the part that kills on a regular basis *does* end at Tabcat Bridge but it begins at Deal's Gap, North Carolina, not Robbinsville. Ethan was on his way to Deal's Gap. He had never been there but he had done his research.

As the crow flies, there are only about six miles between the two points, but with three hundred and eighteen twisting, undulating curves—many of which turn back on themselves—the odometer reading comes out to eleven miles of the most treacherous highway in the United States. There is never a shortage of careless and inept people, so the Dragon feeds well.

The Dragon has been there throughout much of the Earth's history, but it lay dormant for around two hundred million years after the North American and African continents collided to form the Smoky Mountains, a part of the Appalachian chain that runs from Alabama, north through Maine and across the Atlantic to the British Isles.

The elemental stuff of which the chain was forged, according to most geologists, had originated as sediment that accumulated in a shallow sea located between the continents over billions of years, until it was pushed up in that antediluvian cataclysm that twisted and folded the outer crust of the North American continent like wet papier-mâché.

The Appalachians are an old chain as mountains go, worn down by time, lush with vegetation, rife with yet still undiscovered species and flowing with streams and rivers. The Dragon waited quietly as large animals first, then the early human inhabitants of the continent began to wear foot trails through the Smoky Mountains. In the Nineteenth Century, Europeans settlers took the foot trails for themselves and turned them into a rustic roadway for which they charged tolls. All this time, the Dragon waited.

It wasn't until 1934, when road crews laid down the asphalt, officially creating US Highway 129, an artery for the increasing traffic that undulated down the mountain like the serpent it was. Only then did the Dragon got its first real taste of blood, as vehicles with brakes and tires not up to the three hundred and eighteen curves in eleven miles on a grade that drops from nineteen hundred and sixty-two feet above sea level at Deal's Gap to less than four hundred feet above sea level just eleven miles away at Tabcat Bridge—a decline so sharp that even today professional truckers with state-of-the art vehicles avoid if at all possible.

Ethan slowed down, took an interstate ramp at Watts Road in the west end of Knox County and rode into a truck stop to get gasoline and stretch his legs. He circled around past the eighteen wheelers to an area reserved for lesser vehicles. The rumble of his V-Twin cruiser engine slowed, coughed and then died as he stopped by a pump.

To dedicated, almost fanatical riders of American motorcycles, only two machines worthy of notice have ever been manufactured— the Harley-Davidson, which recently celebrated its one hundredth birthday and the Indian. Both machines were born around the turn of the Twentieth Century.

They were fierce competitors and until 1953, when the Indian company went under, leaving Harley-Davidson as the *only* American motorcycle still in production, the oldest in the world. Despite attempts to revive the Indian, it was only between 1999 and 2003 that a bike worthy of the *real* Indian legend was once again briefly available. Ethan had purchased one of the latter-day Indians during the last resurrection.

A cult grew around the Indian, born of scarcity after 1953, and the Indian motorcycle became an icon. They were lovingly rebuilt, discussed and traded by proud owners for almost fifty years until someone bought the Indian name and went back into business for a short time. In the late fifties, after Marlon Brando and Lee Marvin rode onto the silver screen as counter culture heroes in *The Wild Ones* motorcycles replaced the horse and bikers replaced the cowboy as American icons of freedom.

The absolute cornerstone of the one per center movement— that being the name adopted by outlaw bikers of all stripes after an official of the American Motorcycle Association said that ninety-nine percent of all motorcycle riders were law-abiding citizens—was that no self-respecting outlaw would ride a foreign-made motorcycle. The culture that was spawned by *The Wild Ones*, and grew around Harley-Davidson and Indian motorcycles, conveniently overlooked the fact that Brando and Marvin were riding European bikes in that film, with neither a Harley nor Indian in sight.

Ethan knew he was drawing stares because even in a region that draws motorcycle riders of all kinds like moths to a flame, the machine he was riding stood out. It was a 2002 Indian Chief, custom painted orange and white. Everyone who saw it assumed that Ethan had adopted the custom paint job from the University of Tennessee "Big Orange" theme. It wasn't true, though. He was a graduate of Vanderbilt and only vaguely aware of football. He just happened to like orange and white.

Ethan had only recently learned the history of Indian motorcycles. In truth, he hadn't known anything about the history of *any* motorcycle until after Montana left him for a Nashville police officer. He had lived until the age of thirty-three without ever having ridden a motorcycle or even having desired to do so. It was the sting of being called *dull* that had sent him down the path of confrontation with a dragon.

He hadn't gone to work for a week after the split with Montana. He could do that because he owned a company that made specialized computers for people who needed to run better than average graphics systems than most and he didn't answer to many people. Among the feats of courage he had considered before buying the motorcycle were scuba diving in shark-infested waters, sky diving and climbing mountains.

He might have settled on any of the three, had he not seen an Indian motorcycle on display at a mall in Nashville. He had been drawn to it because so many people who seemed to know more about motorcycles than he did were so impressed.

The same day he saw the Indian motorcycle at the mall, he had gone online, found the machine he was now riding, paid $26,000 dollars, had it especially painted and some modifications made, then signed up to take riding lessons from a professional driving school so he could get his license upgraded to ride a motorcycle in Tennessee. It had later occurred to him that signing up for the lessons was the type of thing that had annoyed Montana—his steadfast desire to do things by the numbers. But at least the act of buying the 2002 Indian Chief motorcycle had been on the spur of the moment.

Ethan had found out about the Dragon while researching the kind of activities enjoyed by people who rode motorcycles for fun. The idea of doing *anything* just for fun was in itself a novel idea to a man who carefully planned everything in excruciating detail. Once, he had told Montana that he had never learned to play as a child, but she told him that since his work was the thing he loved most, his entire career was play and he had never learned to work.

The really big bike events in he United States seemed to be in Sturgis, South Dakota and Daytona Beach, Florida. But the Dragon seemed the perfect solution to his problem. It was relatively close to Nashville and he could go after it anytime he wished, not just on a special date

There was another thing that drew him to it, though. People on Indian motorcycles had no doubt challenged the Dragon before the company folded in 1953, but Ethan could find nothing about Indian motorcycle riders doing so since 1999 when the Indian was resurrected for its last five year stint and went out of business again. It might have happened, but he could find no specific account.

Ethan got off the 2002 Indian motorcycle and removed his leather gloves to pump gas. By the time he reached Knoxville, he had noticed that his full body orange and white, custom made leathers were flashier than those worn by most bikers, but he didn't want to take the time to buy new ones. He was committed to having this thing over. The Dragon was waiting.

Ethan had just finished filling his tank when a voice intruded into his thoughts.

"That is one impressive motorcycle." Ethan saw that the man addressing him, was wearing a flat cap and sunglasses, the kind of outfit people wore to drive convertibles—at least in the movies. "You wouldn't be interested in selling it, would you?"

Ethan blinked through his rimless glasses and stared at the man for a few seconds before answering. "No, I wouldn't want to sell it. I've only had it a few months."

"If you ever *do* decide to sell it, could you give me a call first?" The man took a business card out of his shirt pocket and extended it. "I own several businesses here in Knoxville and I collect sports cars and motorcycles. My unlisted cell phone number is on there and I have it on all the time."

"If I decide to sell it, I'll call you." He saw that the man was perhaps in his forties—a decade older than Ethan and deeply tanned, the kind of tan you only see at the beach or coming out of a tanning salon. Ethan was tall, slender and pale from seldom going into the sun.

"That's one of my babies over there." The man was pointing to a small, red sports car and there was a blonde woman who was as tanned as he sitting in it. Ethan wondered at first if he meant the car or the woman, but the man made it clear with the next sentence. "That's a 1951 MGTD roadster, restored to original condition."

Ethan glanced at the card and put it in his shirt pocket. He was not really comfortable chatting with strangers. "I'll certainly call you if I decide to sell it, Mister Jones."

"Any time, day or night and I'll be on the way or have someone on the way with the money. That's a 2002 Indian Chief, isn't it? Probably cost a small fortune." Jones waited and Ethan realized he expected an answer.

"Yes, it's a 2002. I understand the company is out of business and there won't be any more manufactured. It was around $30,000 after the custom paint and modifications, like the orange and white paint."

"I saw the bracket on the handlebars, too. What's it for?" Jones asked.

"It's a mount for a small digital cam. There's a place for another

behind the seat. I carry the cams, just in case I want to record something." *Like maybe myself slaying a dragon. Dull, she called him!*
"It was nice to meet you Mister...?" the man extended his hand.
"Dieumegard. I manufacture specialty computers—in Nashville."
Ethan decided to end the conversation. "Nice meeting you, too. But I have to stop for coffee and a sandwich before I leave Knoxville—if you will excuse me."

Jones apparently caught the drift. "Have a good trip, sir. I hope to hear from you about that motorcycle."

We'll see, Ethan thought, *after I kill the Dragon and drink his blood.*

ETHAN FINALLY STOPPED for a sandwich at Alcoa, Tennessee and mounted his small and very expensive digital cameras on the Indian. He was on US 129, approaching the Tabcat Bridge, called by some the tip of the Dragon's Tail. The Smoky Mountains rose before him in a breathtaking vista. He had been in those mountains many times on the Pigeon Forge, Gatlinburg side, where most of the tourists congregated, but this was his first view from the less visited side. It was spectacular.

He was holding the Indian at a steady fifty miles per hour when he approached the Tabcat Bridge. With his thumb, he switched on his cams a moment before he crossed because he wanted it *all* on record.

Had Ethan not recognized it from pictures on the Internet, it would have held no significance at all. But it was *the* place where the Dragon began and his heart started to pound. Between 1995 and 2004 alone, eleven riders had died challenging the Dragon.

Ethan knew from his research that the unofficial amateur record—kept by a group of riders called The Deals Gap Riding Society—for a round trip from Deal's Gap to Tabcat Bridge and back was eighteen minutes, which came out to a 62 mph average, but he intended to take his time going up and look things over.

The record was unofficial because trying to make or break speed records was illegal, The Tennessee Highway Patrol and local sheriff's department frowned on the paperwork and attendant problems that traffic death's generate. The record had been set in the early nineties when the traffic wasn't nearly as bad as it currently was.

Local riders from the Knoxville and Maryville area, mostly Harley-

Davidson riders, Ethan had contacted through sites on the Internet told him that they no longer challenged the Dragon at all, except in the winter when there were no cowboys and tourists on crotch rockets behaving like idiots. They told Ethan to stay away if he valued life and limb. The Dragon was dangerous enough without worrying about the idiots, too.

Ethan had just started his ascent in mid-afternoon, on a Saturday in June day, when traffic was supposed to be at its peak—which made him one of the idiots to whom they referred. A man with an IQ in the genius range who was about to risk his life in a fool's quest for love certainly could not be classified as rational. And it felt wonderful!

It wasn't like Montana would come back to him if he killed the Dragon and drank its blood. In fact, she probably would not even mourn his passing if the Dragon killed him. But her words had stung him in a way he couldn't define.

"Ethan, you're a very nice man, but you are so damned *dull*. You won't even fight back when I call you names. Living with you would be like eating plain yogurt every day."

"I'm sorry, Montana. I had no idea," he had replied.

"Do you see what I mean, Ethan? Do you see what I *fucking* mean?" It was the last words she had spoken to him.

Her words alone had provoked the purchase of the Indian motorcycle, but it had gotten worse. A week later, she had married an officer with the Nashville Metropolitan Police Department, a member of the SWAT team, no less. The timing seemed to indicate she had been seeing him *before* she left. Ethan had learned about it because there was a story in the *Tennessean* when they had gotten married in a ceremony that had taken place as they, the minister and the witnesses, all floated down from the sky by parachute.

You have to focus, or you won't even make it to the top, Ethan told himself. Stop dwelling on Montana and pay attention to the road. He had slowed to 40 mph, taking the measure of the Dragon. Within the next hour, he expected to be either vindicated of dullness or dead, but he didn't want it to happen before he even reached the head of the Dragon at Deal's Gap.

If he survived the Dragon, he would send Montana and her new husband a copy of his video or whoever recovered his body would. He had prepared a note offering a large reward to whomever delivered it to Montana if the Dragon drank *his* blood. He supposed the elaborate plan was just another example of his dull predictability, but it would not matter either way after he had killed the Dragon.

Ethan suddenly realized what *real* elation was as the 2002 Indian Chief throbbed under him and he traversed the treacherous curves— around the side of the mountains and above ravines that seemed to drop off into nowhere, knowing full well that an encounter with another vehicle of any kind would erase his existence if he or one of them slipped over the center line just a little. And for nothing more than a pointless quest for thrills. Ethan felt *alive*.

Was this how it felt *not* to be dull, not to have prepared for every eventuality? What would it feel like when he came *down* from Deal's Gap at a speed too terrifying to imagine?

That was when Ethan heard screeching tires beyond the curve ahead. He began to brake just as the blue and white motorcycle—the kind riders had to practically lie down on—crossed the road at an angle to him, filling the air with the smell of burning rubber, and vanished into the trees and bushes to Ethan's left.

It happened so fast that Ethan's adrenalin didn't begin to pump because of the close encounter until he had rounded two more curves. By the time he found a place to get off the road and killed the engine, however, he was shaking uncontrollably and had no idea how far he had traveled up the mountain after he saw the blue and white motorcycle vanish into the ravine.

Eventually, he fished out his cell phone and called 911.

"I'VE NEVER SEEN a camera that records this clearly," the young Tennessee State Trooper named Greg Lusk said. "Play it back again."

An ambulance was standing by at the graveled overlook, and a sheriff's department cruiser sat near the highway patrol vehicle. The chatter of emergency radios and the flashing lights had calmed Ethan considerably. Things were under control again. The road was blocked on both sides of the place where the motorcycle had gone over. Because of Ethan's digital recording, the search crews had been able to pinpoint almost the exact scene of the accident.

"It's state of the art technology," Ethan said, resetting the timer to a point just before the moment he had crossed paths with the blue and white motorcycle and its rider.

The two of them watched once more as the curves came and went smoothly on the small screen. It was almost mesmerizing as the line in the center of the road seemed to whip like a yellow ribbon in front of Ethan's Indian motorcycle.

"There, pause it!" Ethan pressed the button and the blue and white motorcycle stopped in mid-frame, a split second before it vanished into the trees. "If you hadn't heard the tires squalling, you might have missed it altogether," Trooper Lusk said. "Whoever was riding that Kawasaki was crazy or suicidal."

"Maybe the brakes failed," Ethan said.

"No, the rider *thought* it was under control. It takes a dim-witted bastard to risk his life and the lives of people he doesn't even know, just to make himself feel like he has a set of balls. These Dragon riders make me sick."

Ethan was about to comment when the trooper's radio crackled. *"Hey Greg, come on down here. We found the Kawasaki."*

"I'll be right there," he said, keying his portable radio. "Come on," the trooper said. "Take a look at what we put up with every day. Your motorcycle will be safe with the deputy watching."

Ten minutes later, Ethan and the trooper were slipping and sliding down the side of as steep ravine. Saplings were broken where the motorcycle had crashed through and the smell of fresh dirt that had been dislodged permeated the air, along with the odor of spilled gasoline. At the bottom, two men in green coveralls that said "rescue" in black letters across the back and another sheriff's deputy were waiting with smiles on their faces." You got two for the price of one, Greg," the deputy said. "You'll be a while doing the two reports."

A mangled motorcycle rested against a large oak tree, partially buried in leaves. But it was red, *not* blue and white, A gold motorcycle helmet with a skull still inside it sat by the red motorcycle as if purposely put there, empty eye sockets appearing to stare towards them. Moldy leather was intermingled with leave, roots and large bones that seemed to have been scattered in a haphazard manner.

"Sonofabitch," the trooper said. "This one must have been here for at least a year."

"Maybe more," one of the men in coveralls said. "The bones are scattered pretty good. Of course, the other motorcycle did part of it. It's over there," he pointed slightly down hill, "and the rider came face down on a protruding rock about ten feet beyond it. His helmet cracked like an egg shell."

"You all right, Mister Dieumegard?" The trooper asked, having apparently noticed the stunned expression on Ethan's face.

"I'm fine," Ethan said.

"Come on," the trooper said, "let's look at the other one."

Ethan wanted to say he had seen enough, but didn't seem to be able to get it out. A few moment's later, he and the trooper were staring down at what had once been a man's face, smeared messily on a mossy rock it had struck before the rest of the body went tumbling on a few feet, where it had landed with arms and legs at unnatural angles.

"If you hadn't seen *this* one, Mister Dieumegard. They both might have stayed down here undiscovered for years. Hell, there may be bodies we don't know about all along Highway 129 between Deal's Gap and the foot of the mountain. A lot of people take on the Dragon and survive. But as you can see, the Dragon drinks its share of blood."

Ethan turned without speaking and climbed out of the ravine. On the road, a tow truck driver wearing University of Tennessee ball cap was preparing to drag the hook and cable from his truck down into the ravine. He nodded at Ethan.

"Can you get another tow truck up here to pick up my motorcycle?" Ethan asked.

"You have a wreck, too?"

"No, my motorcycle is up at the overlook where the ambulance and police car are parked," Ethan said.

"The orange and white Injun? I saw it coming in. Nice ride."

"That's it, can you get another tow truck up here for it?"

"Sure, I can have another truck up here in a few minutes. Somebody told me them Injun motorsickles is bad to break down in the mountains. I'll get on the radio and get a roll back truck on it's way so the motorsickle don't get scratched. You want your bike took on over to Robbinsville?"

"Can I rent a place to stay in Robbinsville, if I need to?" Ethan didn't bother to correct the tow truck driver about the condition of his motorcycle.

"Sure, no problem," the driver answered.

"That's where I want it taken, then."

Ethan walked a few feet from the tow truck and got his cell phone out. He fished the business card the man in Knoxville had given him, punched in the number from the card and waited until it was answered.

142 ... *Things to Do in Knoxville When You're Dead*

"Mister Jones, this is Ethan Dieumegard. You talked to me in Knoxville a few hours back about buying my Indian motorcycle. Are you still interested?".

"Good, if you can have somebody pick up me *and* the motorcycle in Robbinsville, North Carolina and drive me back to Knoxville, you can have it for exactly what I put in it."

"No, *nothing* happened to it. I just have no further use for it."

"You're coming yourself?" Ethan seemed surprised. "Then get started this way and I'll call back with an exact location in Robbinsville as soon as I get there. *Good* I'll see you in about three hours, then."

Ethan ended the call, just as the state trooper came out of the ravine, a little out of breath.

"Trooper Lusk, do you have everything you need from me?"

"I'd like to have a copy of the video. I probably won't need it, but you never know."

"Drive me back up to my motorcycle and I'll give you the entire front digital recorder. All you have to do is download it to a computer. I'm sure somebody in your agency can handle it," Ethan said.

"How will I get the recorder back to you?"

"You keep it. I have another on the motorcycle."

"I'm not supposed to accept gratuities," Trooper Lusk said.

"It can be our secret," Ethan said.

The trooper nodded his head thoughtfully. "Alright. Thank you, Mister Dieumegard. If you don't mind, I'd like to ask you something that's got nothing to do with the accident."

"Go ahead," Ethan said.

"Why were you up here on that big, powerful and expensive motorcycle? You really don't seem like the adventurous type."

"The answer to the question, Trooper Lusk, is that I came up here to meet the Dragon. I did and now I know that I have no business at all with him. And you're right, I'm not adventurous, I'm pretty dull."

"I didn't say you were dull," the trooper shook his head and grinned.

"But I *am* dull. Fortunately, there are women out there that prefer dull over adventurous. When I get back home, I'm going to find one of them."

The Hands of God

THE PAUNCHY OFFICER, wearing a tan and green uniform approached the door of the Toyota Corolla cautiously, his hand hovering near the semi-automatic pistol in his holster. When he was close enough to peer inside, he relaxed a little.

"Afternoon, Reverend. Could I see your license and registration, please."

Carl handed over the license and opened the glove compartment. The officer watched closely as he removed the registration certificate, then handed it over. "Was I speeding, officer? If I was, I apologize. I've just come from a funeral in Middlesboro and I guess my mind was still on it."

"As matter of fact, Reverend. You were doing over sixty-five in a fifty zone. If you'll just set still, I'll have you on your way as soon as I can." The officer backed away from the Corolla, never fully turning around until he got to the cruiser with blue lights flashing on top. He got in, still watching Carl, and spoke into a microphone.

It was a hot, humid day and Carl felt the sweat welling up around the stiff clerical collar. He ran his finger around it, pulling it away from his neck to let the air in. In less than five minutes, the officer once again cautiously approached the Toyota. Carl turned, a smile on his lips and extended his hand for the license.

"Reverend Harkin, I need you to step out of your car please, keeping your hands where I can see them."

"Officer, what seems to be the problem…" Carl began.

"There's not a problem *yet* and I hope there won't be, Reverend. Just step out of the car and step back behind your vehicle to get us out of the road. Somebody else might speed through here, not payin' attention."

Carl did as he was told and the officer once more walked backwards until both of them were behind the Corolla. "Now, Reverend, turn and face your car. Put your hands on the trunk lid, step back two steps and spread your legs wide."

"Officer is this *necessary* for a simple case of speeding? I live one county over and I've lived there for over thirty years. You can easily check…"

"I *will* check. Now do exactly as I said."

Carl put his hands on the trunk lid of his car. The dark maroon paint was rapidly soaking up sunlight and it was almost uncomfortably warm. He stepped back two steps and spread his legs into an awkward pose. It became even more awkward as the officer put his legs between Carl's ankles and kicked them apart, leaving him barely enough room to hold on to the trunk lid.

Almost immediately he felt intrusive, impersonal hands, starting at his ankles and carefully touching him on both sides of his legs, all the way up to the crotch, where one hand paused long enough to ascertain that he had no weapon hidden near his genitals. The hands continued up his body, stopping at the belt line to feel inside the top of his trousers.

Just when he thought the humiliation was over, the officer took his left hand and pulled it behind his back. Stunned, Carl felt metal handcuffs and heard the ratchets close. Before he could protest, his other hand was also cuffed behind him and the officer helped him stand erect by grasping the collar of his lightweight sports jacket.

"Could you at least put these cuffs in front? It's *very* uncomfortable like this."

"Sorry, Reverend. Handcuffs are not designed for comfort and you might as well not be wearin' any if your hands are in front. A man can do almost anything when he's cuffed to the front that he can do without cuffs. Now, let's walk back to my cruiser and get in where it's air-conditioned."

"Will you tell me what this is all about," Carl asked as he was being guided into the back seat of the cruiser. "Watch your head," the officer said, placing his hand on Carl's head at the same moment. The back door closed and the officer got into the front seat and closed his door.

"Your Tennessee drivers license is revoked for failure to appear on a traffic citation in Gadsen, Alabama," the officer said, removing his lightweight straw Stetson. Carl saw that the man was going bald at the crown.

"I mailed in the money for that citation and I have the cancelled check at home," Carl said. "This is ridiculous! There was no need to handcuff me, even if there's been a clerical error in Alabama. You could write me a citation."

"Reverend, do you see the flaw in the logic of writin' a citation to a man who didn't show up for court the last time he got a citation?"

"I told you I paid that ticket! Officer, I need your name and badge number." Carl felt ridiculous, even as he said it.

"My name is Charles Campbell and my badge number is number *one* because I'm the sheriff of this county," he answered, picking up his microphone. "Dispatch, this is Unit One. I need a wrecker at this location."

"You're towing my car?"

"Yes I am, Reverend. I can't leave it by the road. Somethin' might happen to it."

Carl took a deep breath and blew it out, struggling for self control. "Sheriff, you don't have to call me *reverend*. I'm an Episcopal priest, *the* Reverend Carl Harkin." Carl realized how arrogant he sounded but before he could correct himself, the sheriff responded.

"No offense meant. What should I call you?" the Sheriff turned in the seat and, close up, Carl saw that he was at least in his fifties, though he had appeared younger in the hat.

"Mr. Harkin or Father Harkin, or just Carl, if you prefer. I didn't mean to be rude, but it has been a bad day for me."

"*Harkin*. That's an Arab name isn't it?" The sheriff said, almost matter-of-factly.

"I don't know. I've heard that and I've also heard it may be Celtic, Irish or Scots. "Is that what this is about? Am I being profiled because of my name?"

"No, Mr. Harkin, you have not been profiled. I didn't even *know* your name until you came speedin' through my county, driving on a revoked license."

"I'm sorry, Sheriff, I shouldn't have said that. The funeral I attended was for a close friend of mine from seminary, and…"

"Excuse me, Mr. Harkin, your wrecker is here and I need to sign your car over to the driver," the Sheriff said, opening the door and letting in a blast of hot air.

...

THE JAIL WAS in the basement of the courthouse and it had obviously been around a while. Carl shuddered as the metal door clanged behind him. Suddenly he remembered what was meant by the term *slammer.* "Have a seat at the table and I'll be back in a minute. I just got one jailer on duty and he's dispatchin' too. Make yourself comfortable and I'll try to get through this as fast as I can."

The sheriff went down a hallway to the right of the table. Carl heard a filing cabinet open and the sheriff returned in a minute or two carrying a pad that looked like some kind of official report form.

"Can I get you something to drink, Mr. Harkin? We ain't got much in the way of amenities but I'll rustle up somethin' if you like."

"As matter of fact, I'm a diabetic and some juice or a soft drink would be nice. It was almost time for lunch and I think my blood sugar's a little low," Carl said.

Once more the sheriff got up and lumbered down the same hallway. This time, Carl heard glass clinking, then a refrigerator opening.

"I hope grape juice is all right," the sheriff said as he came back through the door and took a seat at the table. He set a tumbler on the table for Carl and it was half filled with the purple liquid. Carl picked it up and took a sip. It felt good on his tongue and was very sweet.

"I didn't think glass was allowed in a jail, Sheriff...I mean, the possibility of making a weapon. That's what I've heard, anyway."

The sheriff seemed amused. "Well, Mr. Harkin, I wouldn't allow glass back in the cell block, but you said you needed a drink and that's what my wife left out for me today. This is a small operation."

"I didn't mean to sound condescending, Sheriff. I've never been in jail before," Carl said quickly. No reason to antagonize him. Other than having arrested Carl for a minor offense, he was a pleasant enough man.

"No offense taken, Mr. Harkin, I know I'm a backwoods lawman in a tiny little town." The Sheriff was copying the information from Carl's driver's license on to the form.

"I'd guess you don't get many Episcopalians in here do you, Sheriff. *Damn!* Carl thought, *I seemed determined to insult this man.*

"Well, I guess we might have a few Episcopalians around here, but the closest Episcopal church is in Claiborne County. Mostly Baptists here, with a few Methodists and a few Church of God people mixed in. I serve as a deacon, myself. I'm Baptist."

"Sheriff, I didn't mean..."

"No offense taken, Mr. Harkin." Once more there was amusement in the big lawman's eyes. "Like, I said. I know this is backwoods country. But I ain't Sheriff Andy of Mayberry, either."

Carl decided to keep quiet, pay his fine and be on his way. It was annoying, but the man was doing his job and being polite about it and Carl knew he hadn't been at his sharpest today. He decided not to push his luck by talking too much.

"OK, Mr. Harkin. That takes care of the paperwork. Let's get your picture and fingerprints and we'll take you upstairs and you can have a trial, or let he judge set your bond and set a trial date if you want to get a lawyer and contest the charge."

"Fingerprints? Pictures? For a traffic offense?"

"Rules are the same for everybody, Mr. Harkin. You can get jail time for drivin' on a revoked license. It's mandatory if you're convicted—though the judge will probably let you slide if there's a good reason."

"You haven't read me my rights, Sheriff and I haven't talked to my attorney. We don't go any further until I *do* talk to him."

"Mr. Harkin, I *saw* you commit the offense, so I didn't have to read your rights because it's a misdemeanor and I didn't need to question you." The big lawman seemed genuinely surprised. "Just cooperate and you'll be out of here in thirty minutes."

"I want my attorney, Sheriff."

"CARL, I HOPE you had a very good reason for interrupting my tennis match. I was winning, and pastor or not, if you've dragged me all the way across two counties on some silly principle..." Larry Lagerfield was still dressed in his tennis clothes—a blue polo shirt, white shorts, athletic shoes and the entire outfit topped off with a visor.

"It's *not* a silly principle, Larry. If he takes my fingerprints, my life as I know it now is over," Carl said quietly.

"You're *serious* aren't you, Carl?" Lagerfield was suddenly all business. "Tell me about it and keep your voice low. I don't think this place is high tech enough to be wired for sound, but you never know."

"OK, here it is..." Carl took a deep breath. "In 1969, a group of people from the Weatherman faction of Students for a Democratic Society robbed a bank in New Jersey. A security guard was killed. Later one of the bank robbers was killed in a gunfight with police and one was captured."

"Carl, are you trying to tell me..."

"Yes, Larry. The name I was born with was James Bukowski. I was sentenced to life in prison and I escaped while I was being transported from the court to prison."

"I remember reading about it," Larry said. "You're *the* Jimmy Bukowski. You were on the FBI's most wanted list for years. Jesus, Carl! I don't know what to say."

"Say you can get me out of here without my fingerprints being taken."

Larry Lagerfield inhaled and then exhaled slowly. "Did Sarah know the truth?"

"Yes, Larry. And until just now, she was the only person who *ever* knew. That's one reason I never married again after she died. I couldn't put another woman in that position and I couldn't keep something like that from a woman I loved enough to marry."

"How did you vanish, Carl? I remember that the manhunt was massive," Larry took out a handkerchief and wiped sweat from his forehead. "You don't have to answer that, Carl."

"We have lawyer-client privilege here, so I don't care to tell you. I went to the one place where the authorities never thought to look. I walked into an Army recruiter's office with the identity of a baby who died the year I was born and six months later, I was in the Republic of Vietnam as an infantryman.

"I stayed away from military jobs that would have required a security clearance. I also picked up a Silver Star, which meant something back then. It helped me sail through college on the old GI Bill and then seminary."

"You won a Silver Star in Vietnam, Carl? Jesus, what else don't I know about you?" the lawyer asked.

"Well, for the last thirty years, you pretty much know everything about The Reverend Carl Harkin. Now you know about a stupid kid named Jimmy Bukowski. Can you get me out of here without being fingerprinted?"

"Speaking strictly from a point of law, I can't. This Sheriff went by the book, had every legal reason to arrest you. But I came prepared for that eventuality. That's why I'm so expensive." The lawyer opened his leather briefcase that had a shoulder strap rather than a hand-grip, and took out a book.

"You're going to appeal to his literary side? I don't think that will work here, Larry."

"That you're the author of a religious bestseller that the President of the United States has quoted from will be the opening gambit. But I'm also going to give a sound and light show, maybe even call some people in powerful places."

"Larry, I don't think this sheriff is the kind of man who is easily impressed or scared," Carl said.

"Well, we're about to find out," the lawyer said.

As THEY PULLED away from the jail in Lagerfield's Lincoln Navigator, the tension seemed to drain from Carl's body. He looked at the citation the sheriff had written as if it were a reprieve from disaster, because it was.

"Larry, exactly what did you say to make him change his mind?

"Well, I started by promising to turn your arrest into a public spectacle. I asked him if he really wanted the publicity he would get from holding a man of the cloth over a clerical misunderstanding in Alabama—a man who also happens to be a best-selling author read by the President, the head of a foundation that takes in kids who have no place to go and a man with a lawyer who has coffee with the Governor, sometimes.

"He held out until I told him how much money this county might have to spend defending his actions and asked how the County Commission and Mayor would feel about it. Or more importantly, how the voters would feel about it when they found out that money budgeted for schools was being spent because of a lapse in judgment on his part.

"I think that was the tie-breaker, because that's when Sheriff Andy fetched the citation book and told his deputy to get your signature and turn you loose." Lagerfield said. "He also said he'd call and have your car released from the wrecker service that towed it."

"I don't believe he's the ignorant rube you think he is, Larry. There wasn't any bluster or uncertainty about him. He seemed to be a good man, doing his job."

"Well, it doesn't matter now. You're sprung and he didn't get your fingerprints. I expected you to be elated, Father Carl."

"I guess the stress of the day has caught up with me. Thanks, Larry."

"Wait until you get the bill before you say thanks, Carl." The lawyer chuckled at his own wit.

CARL HARKIN SWALLOWED hard as the uniformed deputy knocked on the door, marked "Sheriff." A moment later, a voice answered from inside. "Come in."

The deputy opened the door and stepped out of Carl's way. The burly sheriff with thinning hair looked up with a faint smile. "You're early, Mr. Harkin. Your court date on the speedin' ticket won't be heard until next Monday. "Course, if you like we can go up and let the judge hear it in chambers. He's here today.

"Oh, I read the book your lawyer left. I won't claim to understand all the theology, but I do understand the idea that God has no hands on Earth except us. And I looked up your inspiration, Saint Teresa, at the library. I was very impressed, and if you will, I'd like to have your autograph on my copy of *We Are the Hands of God*. I never met a famous author before. Sit down, Mr. Harkin take a load off."

"I'll be glad to sign your book Sheriff, but I don't think you'll want it after I tell you what I've come to say."

"And what's that, Mr. Harkin?"

"To begin with, I wasn't born with the name Carl Harkin."

"Oh, *that's* what you came to tell me. I appreciate the candor but I already knew." The big man began to dig around on his cluttered desk.

"I beg your pardon, Sheriff. But you couldn't possibly know because you didn't get my fingerprints."

The Sheriff found what he was looking for. He handed a manila file to Carl across the desk. "I got your prints off the glass you drank the juice out of. Crime scene technician was one of the jobs I did with the Nashville Police Department before I retired and came home to run for office. It's also the reason I didn't mind turnin' you loose with a citation. I knew I could lay my hands on you if I wanted to."

Carl opened the folder and saw a picture of himself at twenty, bearded and with shaggy hair. It was a mug shot from New Jersey, and copies of all the reports that went along with his arrest there for armed robbery and murder committed in the commission of a felony.

"It usually takes a while to run a partial set of prints, but I have a friend in the National Security Agency. We worked together in the Army Security Agency back in the sixties. He stayed on with the government and I went to Nashville and became a cop. Prints are quicker to run when you have a discrete access to *that* kind of files. Nobody knows about this except him and me—and now you."

"When were you coming after me, Sheriff?" Carl asked.

"I had already decided I *wasn't* coming after you, assumin' you showed up and paid your fine. When you walked in this room to confess, it was just a bonus, an assurance that I had made the right decision. As far as I'm concerned, Jimmy Bukowski the Weatherman revolutionist died when Carl Harkin joined the Army and went to Vietnam. My friend has access to the military data base, too. They didn't give out Silver Stars in Cracker Jack boxes."

"I don't know what to say, Sheriff Campbell. I obviously underestimated you. I apologize."

The Sheriff leaned back in his chair and smiled. "Well, your jackleg lawyer did, but you were polite enough."

"Was my military record what made you decide to...give me a break? I wasn't brave, you know. I was terrified and I didn't *deserve* that medal."

"Heroes are *always* terrified Father Harkin. That's why they're heroes. But the medal wasn't the only reason. I was impressed by your book and what you've done with your life, since then. And I'm a deacon in the Baptist Church. We believe in deathbed conversions, you know. *Converted* means "turned around," if I remember correctly, and if ever a man turned around, you did."

"Besides, you didn't pull the trigger in that robbery. If you had, my decision would have required more thought."

"Sheriff, I'm speechless and I'm appreciative...but I still want to turn myself in. Jimmy Bukowski will always be out there. I've been living a lie for thirty years and I can't deal with it, any more."

"Father Harkin, I thought you might feel that way. And it if you still want to turn yourself in, you can go to the FBI office in Knoxville. But you've managed to go almost thirty years without bein' arrested, and if you keep your traffic citations paid, the occasion will probably never arise again for you to be printed. Personally, I think you ought to leave Jimmy Bukowski where you left him. You've done your time in Purgatory."

"Episcopalians don't believe in Purgatory, Sheriff Campbell. That's a Roman Catholic doctrine."

"I'm just a simple man, a Baptist Deacon workin' on a second pension to supplement my pension from Nashville. But those of us who work in law enforcement find out early that the law and justice ain't always the same thing. Once in a while, we get a chance to actually administer justice instead of just enforcin' rules.

"Now, if you'll sign this book, we'll go up and see the judge so you can pay your ticket for speedin'. You can take Jimmy Bukowski's file and do whatever you think is best because I have no use for it."

Carl Harkin, stood up and took the copy of his book from Sheriff Campbell. He opened it to the title page and wrote: *To Sheriff Charles Campbell, with gratitude. From the Rev. Carl Harkin.*

The big Sheriff took the book and read the inscription: "Thank you, Father Harkin. I'll treasure the book."

"And thank you, Sheriff." Carl picked up the Bukowski file. He knew he was in for a sleepless night.

The Price of Safety

"Chief, I'd like to help you out but I have to make a profit. There was only a thousand of these Desert Storm limited edition Glock 17s made and the price ain't goin' down none."

Assistant Chief Ronald Caputo was in a grand mood and ready to haggle. He had just received four contributors' copies of *Police Life and Times*, with an article he had written. He was so proud of it, he had left a copy on the sheriff's desk that morning. The editors at the magazine had no way of knowing that he was an office pogue, who had never heard a shot fired in anger. His title, "Deputy Chief, Training Division," looked impressive on the by-line.

"Come on Alvin, I spend a lot of money here and I send people to you. In fact, I'll give you a *special* promotion during in-service training this year. All the officers *have* to take my classes to stay certified as cops in Tennessee. My men love me and I have a lot of influence with them. You can give me at least *three*-hundred on my Glock 27. I've got it in the car. I'm ready to deal."

"Chief, I can't *give* the Glock 27s away right now." *Besides, I know what the men you train say about you.* Unlike the editors at *Police Life and Times*, Al Keck knew that not only did the men hate Caputo, but that the "true life" incidents he had taken to writing and talking about lately, were somebody else's experiences, gleaned from police reports he read every day as a part of his job as a training officer. He had no real street experiences because he had worked as a fingerprint technician for the New York City Police Department during his two years there.

Caputo looked like a movie poster cop, though—tall, broad shouldered, with perfectly styled black, wavy hair, and his uniforms were always immaculate, which was not surprising since he never did anything to dirty them. The previous sheriff had been so impressed with his looks, he had hired him on the spot and made him a training officer. But the real cops had figured him out the first year.

"You cops *always* want a bargain," Al said, a little more sharply than he had meant. "Of course, you *deserve* special treatment for layin' yer lives on the line every day. *Besides, even an idiot like you might accidentally cause problems for a licensed gun dealer*, Al thought to himself.

"But Al, I buy a *lot* of guns from you. Come on and help me out here." Caputo's Brooklyn accent was still thick after ten years in Knoxville, Tennessee.

"Ron, why do you even *want* this special edition Glock. You're not a collector. You carry everything you buy. All you're gonna do is devalue this pistol and lose money on it when you trade it in. It's still in the box with the authentication."

"Al, I just want it, that's all I can say. I don't know why." It wasn't true. Caputo had already imagined the line in which he would use it when he finished the book of his police experiences that had all happened to someone else. *"I put my hand on the Glock 17 Desert Storm edition and dared him with my eyes to draw his own pistol..."*

"Maybe, I can kick it up by fifty bucks, but that's the final offer, Ron. I wanna help, but I run a business here." Al hung his big belly over the glass counter-top, which contained a smorgasbord of weapons from all over the world—everything from replicated Colt Peacemakers to a double-barreled Saturday night special that barely met the legal definition of a handgun and fired .410 shotgun shells, assuming anyone was stupid enough to actually fire a weapon purchased new for under fifty dollars.

"Done," Caputo said. He felt elated, confident of his haggling ability. Al also felt elated because he had been willing to give Caputo a much better deal. The limited edition Glock had not increased in value as much as the manufacturer had hoped. There is apparently something about an ugly but terribly efficient pistol, which does not lend itself to ornate engraving. As they were each feeling elation, the transaction suddenly became moot as the front door was kicked open.

"Both of you git yer fuckin' hands up!"

Caputo raised his hands, instantly. He prayed that it was a police officer, playing a trick. To his horror, a man with a ski mask over his face, stepped up to the counter and put a sawed-off 12 gauge shotgun to the deputy chief's impeccably groomed head.

"I don't keep no cash on hand," Al said.

"I *know* that, old man. I ain't lookin' for cash. I want all the nine millimeter pistols out of the case, and all the nine millimeter ammunition off your shelf. Don't think about pushin' no alarm button. Now!" He tossed two canvas bags on the counter. Though the fog of sheer terror, Caputo noted that the bags were from the Knox County Library.

Al, picked up the two bags and began to fill one of them with pistols. After all, the expensive weapons were in the vault and he was insured. Apparently the robber was interested only in getting in and out quickly and realized he could only carry so much. Outside, Al saw an old white Oldsmobile with another masked person behind the wheel. The car was smoking badly.

"That a nine millimeter you're carryin' pretty boy?" the man asked, lightly touching Caputo's cheek with the shotgun

"No…" Caputo's mouth was dry. "It's a Glock .40 caliber."

"Unsnap the holster and take the pistol out with two fingers. I'll take it, anyway. Don't want you shootin' at us as we leave."

"It belongs to the Knox County Sheriff's Department," Caputo heard himself say with a thrill of terror. It's really going to upset the sheriff if you take it."

"But *you* don't care do ya, pretty boy." The man jabbed him with the shotgun on the cheek bone, hard.

"No…not at all," Caputo croaked out, putting the pistol delicately on the glass counter top.

"Hurry up, old man!" Al put the last of the nine millimeter ammunition, fifty to a box, in the bag and grunted as he put it on the counter.

"Put the cop's pistol in one of the bags."

Al did as he was told. The masked man snaked his arm through the carry straps, hefted the weight with one arm and backed up to the door.

"Don't move for two minutes. There's a man with a rifle watching from across the street. It's been nice doin' business with both of you."

Second's later, the car squalled away.

"I doubt there's anybody across the street with a rifle," Al said, "but I ain't takin' any chances. I'm insured."

Caputo was silent. He knew he'd be filling out paperwork all afternoon, explaining why he had lost his pistol, why he hadn't gotten a good description of the robber or even a tag number—though even an office pogue like him knew the car had probably already been abandoned, even as they waited for the two minutes to elapse.

He would later refuse an interview to the news media, but the story would make page one of the *Knoxville News Sentinel* and first story status on every local television station. A high-ranking cop being robbed of his weapon was too good to pass up. All his past humiliation would seem inconsequential in light of what had just happened.

Back at headquarters, the sheriff was reading his article. All the patrolmen, he knew, would also read it, especially after they found out about the robbery. The article was entitled, "Constant Vigilance: The Officer's Key to Survival."

Printed in the United States
78253LV00006B/187-201